The Oddities ar
b.

MW01128075

Acknowledgements

The residents and visitors of Key West were instrumental in creating the inspiration for this book. Likewise were the institutions, such as The Cork and Stogie, The Green Parrot, The Porch, Grunts, Captain Tony's, Rick's, Two Friends, The Bait Shop, Conch Republic Seafood, The Boat House, and of course, The Conch Rock Shanty. The atmospheres and characters who inhabited these places and establishments provided much of the inspiration for this book. Additionally, the island of Key West, as well as the rest of the Keys in the archipelago of the Conch Republic stretching from Elliot Key, just north of Key Largo, to The Dry Tortugas, including all of the keys in the Florida Bay/Gulf of Mexico. This area has a very strong creative energy, for which I am forever grateful.

Disclaimer

This is a book of fiction. Although many real life people inspired the book, all characters within the work are fictitious.

Dedication

This book is dedicated to Danielle (Dani) Hoy. Whose love, patience, and assistance could only be expressed and measured on the Richter Scale.

Thank you Dani!!!! I love you!

Table of contents

Time Traveler • 1 • The Dream

It wasn't as though he had any control over it. When the phenomenon started, he was asleep. That first time, when he woke, it seemed like such a vivid dream. On the other hand, it seemed like it was just too real and he didn't feel rested at all. As a matter of fact, he was quite tired! Odder than that, he felt the mild effects of alcohol from the night before, yet he hadn't drunk anything at all. In his quandary, the day went on and the memory was not at all like that of a regular dream that fades as the day and minutes went on. It was so real. The people he met during the experience were so much in the flesh, as were the experiences. The other odd thing was that the "dream" occurred in the town he lived in, albeit many years prior. Here he was in the Twenty-First century, but the dream took place in the 1930's. It was so peculiar, bizarre even. If there ever was an appropriate word for it, bizarre was indeed the correct word.

Key West. That was the town of choice five years ago. It was a small city on the outer limits of the U.S., an island town over one hundred miles out to sea. Curiously enough it's a city you can drive to, island hopping across forty-five bridges that link the archipelago coral chain of islands known as The Florida Keys.

His name was Mark Straight and he had been around the world several times in his lifetime, approaching his fourth decade. He certainly was no green traveler. He had seen the good, the bad, and the evil and decided the bad and the evil were not his cup of tea. Key West offered the sanctuary he had been seeking. Key West wasn't the real world. It was isolated and had a mentality of its own. The Keys in general, be it Key West, Key Largo or The Dry Tortugas for that matter, had an entirely different way of life than the rest of the United States. Back in 1982, the island chain had actually seceded from the U.S. in a mock uprising. Declaring themselves independent, they coined The Conch Republic as the name for their brave new world. This was a cornerstone, long overdue, that reflected the independence of the islands and the very different mentality that they encompassed. In many cases, if something could be warped into a farce, the Conch Republic is where it was found. Laughter was the order of the day and this is what Mark craved at this juncture in his life. He moved and settled in the capital of The Conch Republic, Key West, five years ago.

At this stage of the game, he knew the island like the back of his hand. He learned all of the insights through the tradition of experience. For instance, he knew Key West is a town where you drive your car only out of necessity. Parking is too much of a nuisance. No, you generally either walk or ride a bike unless you're hauling goods, the vehicle stays parked.

Consequently, one tends to read between the lines as far as the geographical nuances go. When one walks or rides a bike innuendos pave the path. The town is loaded with nooks and crannies that you would never see driving in a car. As a matter of fact, even riding a bike, you tend to miss about fifty percent of what you would see walking. While Mark did a good deal of bike riding, he also did a lot of walking. He knew this town inside out.

Key West is a town unlike its northern neighbor Miami, it preserves its past. Miami pledges its allegiance to the bulldozer and its trusty assistant, the wrecking ball. Key West has ordinances set out that forbid structures being torn down. It is permissible to restore older buildings, and the funny thing about this is that the restored versions tend to be much more opulent than the originals. It's all good, albeit there being more renovations rather than restorations, but the point, is that the town today looks quite the same as it did over one-hundred years ago.

In his peculiar sleeping experience, Mark found himself knowing points of interest and living where he currently lived, albeit in a different setting. Unlike regular dreams, there was no jumping from one point to another. If he was going from one point to another, there was time and traveling involved, just as in real life. The oddest thing was that it seemed exactly like real life.

Mark, in conscious life, worked as a bartender making exotic drinks at an old, classic, Victorian bar in a mansion which dates from the

1840's, The Side Car. He also works in another bar which specializes in local beers from around the world, as well as wine and cigars, The Cork and Stogie.

As he rode his bike to work to the Victorian bar that morning, all he could think about was the very peculiar dream he had. The more he thought about it, the more puzzling it seemed. He actually had seen this very Victorian mansion in the dream, however, in the 1930's, it was a home and office of a well-known doctor.

The dream started with Mark tending bar at a restaurant on lower Duval Street, the main street in Key West, called The Victoria Restaurant. When the dream started, Mark was tending bar and mixing, fittingly enough, an Old Fashioned. As he turned to his left, he found himself facing his fellow bartender, Freddy. Freddy was quite busy vigorously shaking a whiskey sour.

"Got yours done? Glades is ready," stated Freddy.

"All set. Here you go," replied Mark, putting his drink on Glades' tray. It was odd indeed. Suddenly, there he was in a rush hour, in the midst of mixing cocktails, yet thinking nothing of it at all. There was a job to be done. At that moment, all he knew was that he was mixing an Old Fashioned and the waitress was waiting. In this dream, he also knew everyone well.

Glades smiled. She looked like one of the Andrews Sisters. Her hair was up in a bon vivant style. Her outfit was much more like an old time nurse's ensemble. White, with red ruffles, It appeared to be full of starch and possessed the flexibility of cardboard. Mark marveled at how quickly she scooted from the bar with the drinks in that stiff contraption she was wearing.

A "contraption" was the right word, as well. After she delivered the drinks to the table she was serving, she approached the kitchen, stopped and bent over to pick up a stray napkin. Mark watched her and was amazed to see what appeared to be the equivalent of a suspension bridge with straps going this way and that, under her dress. She looked back to see him looking at her in amazement, then quickly composed herself and rushed into the kitchen, nervously pulling her compact out, to check her makeup and lipstick, as she whisked through the swing doors of the bustling kitchen.

Mark didn't realize it, but that was how she wanted it to look. She was looking behind her to see if Mark was still looking. He was and she smiled to herself. Curiously, Mark found Glades to be indeed quite attractive. He even had a hankering to try out as a Flying Walenda high-wire act and go for a swing on Glades' trapeze.

Glades Valdez was twenty-six. Her parents came from Cuba before she was born and after she was conceived in Cuba. She would joke "Hecho en Cuba, nacido en U.S.A." Which translates into "Made in Cuba, born in the U.S.A." She spoke Spanish with a Cuban accent and English with what is known as a Conch accent. Throughout the Florida Keys, the people born on the islands call themselves "Conchs," a throwback from the original settlers who came from the Bahamas and referred to themselves after the crustacean prior to emigrating to the Keys.

The Conch accent is a unique one. It sounds a lot like if Brooklyn mated with Alabama. Glades and Fred had Conch accents. Mark, however, was different. He was from Connecticut.

"I think that Glades has a thing for you, Bubba," said Freddy. The colloquial term "Bubba" being the term for someone who was "one of them."

"Seriously?" replied Mark.

"Uhm-Humm! No doubt about it. Hey, you want to hit The Blind Pig after we get off?"

"The Blind Pig? Sounds great I could use a cocktail made for me for once."

The Blind Pig was actually its old name from when it was a speakeasy, but that was only a few years before. In this town, old names are hard to shake and new names take a while to settle into the place. Mark looked at a paper a patron left on the bar. March 16th, 1935 was the date.

"1935? How did I get here?" Mark was thinking. He looked around and immediately knew where he was. He was in Sloppy Joe's, but it looked a bit different. There were no fish hanging on the walls. There was the men's room where the kitchen had been. The tables were all covered in white linen with matching napkins. When he looked up he saw the sign "Victoria Restaurant."

Every now and then one realizes that they are in a dream while in the dream. This was now dawning on Mark.

"This is one hell of a dream," he was thinking. Then he thought, "I'm just going to roll with this. It could be fun!" Indeed, it was one of those very rare occasions where one actually realizes they are, in fact, in a dream.

He and Freddy finished up and, unlike a dream, it was as though it was in real time. It took an hour to clean and set up the bar for the next day. The bottles were all an older style, ornate and heavy, with beautiful labels. The fixtures were also heavy and quite stylish; and when he turned on the water, unlike a regular dream, he could feel it.

When they left, Freddy subtly leads them in a brisk walk across Duval Street to the other side and the corner of Greene Street. Arriving at the corner, Mark stopped dead in his tracks. He stared at the sign on the bar hanging over the sidewalk.

Freddy, impatient, took a few more steps and turned around and said "Hey! What are you stopping for? Let's get a beer!"

Mark looked at the sign. He knew the place as Captain Tony's, but there it was, plain as day, reading "Sloppy Joe's". Everyone in town today knows that Captain Tony's was the original Sloppy Joe's.

Sloppy Joe's is an institution after all. It had been in this location from 1933 to 1937. Before that it was the speakeasy known as The Blind Pig.

They walked through the open French doors. The layout was different than he knew it. Yes, there was the hanging tree growing through the middle of the bar, however, the bar was along the left wall, with booths in the back. In what he knew as the pool room, there was a dance floor instead. The sign read "The Silver Slipper." Couples were dancing to Cuban music of the era, blaring out of a phonograph cone speaker from a 78 record.

The bar was dark. The only light seemed as though it was from the street lights outside.

"Hey! Grab us a couple of Royals from Skinner!" hollered Freddy, as he hurried to the men's room. Mark had seen a local beer named Royal back at the Victoria, so Skinner must be the bartender.

Skinner was a large black man, no less than three hundred pounds. He had a big grin on his face, yet at the same time, you could tell he kept a little bit in reserve, just in case. In a bar like this, that "just in case" most likely happened several times a day.

Mark walked up to the bar casually, but at a deliberate pace. "Hey Skinner, how are you?"

Skinner replied "Alright! You Mark? What will you be having tonight?" It was funny because everyone in this dream knew him, and he felt like he knew them.

"Could I get two Royals?"

Skinner reached down into the ice box and pulled out two cans of Royal beer. They were curious cans of the era, with a cone shaped top and a screw cap. Skinner opened them both and set them on the bar.

"That'll be twelve cents, Mark," uttered Skinner

Surprised, Mark laughed shook his head and asked "Twelve cents?" Beers started at five dollars back in the Twenty-First-Century.

"Yeah, they went up a penny from last week."

He reached into his pocket and pulled out a buffalo nickel and a mercury dime. "Here you go, keep the change.":

Skimmer smiled, nodded and then moved on to the next customer.

Freddy came back and Mark said to him, "Price of beer is up to six cents. I got this round, but the next one's on you."

"Six cents! What's the world coming to?" Freddy exclaimed half in surprise half in jest.

"Just think, by the Twenty-First century they'll probably be five bucks each," Mark said in a little tongue-in-cheek joke to himself.

"Can you imagine? No, that'll never happen, Five bucks a beer! HA HA HA!" replied Freddy, his Conch accent heavy and his a laugh loud.

Frederick "Freddy" Carpenter. He was a little younger than Mark, at thirty-three. He stood around five-seven, and maybe one hundred and forty-five pounds. He was full of energy, and easily excited about things in general. Born to a well to do and long established family in town, he nonetheless went out on his own instead of going into the family business. He loved his family but loved his independence more. He loved a good bar and this was his favorite. Freddy took a hard swig of his Royal, directly from the can. "Ahhhh! Now that's what I've been waiting for!"

To Mark's sophisticated palate, this Royal beer was actually a decent beer. It was an all malt pilsner product brewed in Key West. Not bad. He and Freddy joked for a bit, drinking a few beers when Freddy nudged Mark and used his eyes to point to the side. Taking his cue, Mark turned around to see Glades and Erica, one of her girlfriends, walking through the front door.

They went directly for Mark and Freddy and gave them a friendly greeting. The girls ordered Manhattans, and the conversation took off from there. They first started talking about their common bond, working at the Victoria. Co-workers, customers, order mix ups. Mark thought that in all these years, the restaurant business never changes. After a bit, Mark suggested to Glades "Let's go cut a rug at the Silver Slipper!" Glades thought it was a great idea, agreeing enthusiastically.

The Silver Slipper was off to the side and a couple of steps down. As things turned out, Mark was quite a dancer, as was Glades, and they made quite a hit with the crowd on the dance floor. It got to the point that on one energetic number the couples on the dance floor went off to the side and clapped to the rhythm of the beat of the music, cheering on Mark and Glades as they burnt the carpet to everyone's enjoyment.

It was a great evening. When they stopped dancing they found that Freddy and Erica were no longer in the bar. He offered Glades another drink, but he had run out of change, so he pulled out his wallet and found it with several dollar bills from a different era than he was accustomed. He gave Skinner one and Skinner gave him the change, the beer, and the cocktail.

After a couple more libations, Mark offered to see Glades home. She didn't live far away, just a few blocks down on Fishbone Lane, which ran between Eaton and Caroline Streets. He knew it as Peacon Lane. It wasn't far from where the shrimpers hung out and that was no place for a girl to go at night. She was a few blocks west of there, but Mark thought it best to walk her home.

Shrimpers were about as rough a crew as one would find. They'd just as quickly shake your hand with a warm greeting, as they would knocking your lights out. The latter happened when they were

drinking. It was nighttime and a shrimper's bar, the Bucket Of
Blood, was just a couple of block's down from where Glades lived.
Mark would see her home at this hour.

Glades had a room above the corner store, which had a rear entrance.
She jokingly called it The Pelican's Nest. When they got there,
Glades said "I know you are acquainted with a lot of old things.
Collectible antiques and haberdashery-like things. I inherited this
brooch and maybe you can give me some advice on it."

"I'd be happy to. When would you like me to look at it?"

"Well, you're here right now. I know it's late, but it will only take a
few minutes."

"Sure," Mark said, in a matter of fact fashion.

"Good! Come on, let me show you!" she said happily.

They went inside to review the brooch. It was classic and ornate.
Mark was guessing it may have been around one hundred years old.
He was impressed with it. Gauging it against drinking five cent beer,
he guessed it may be worth around twenty-five dollars. Glades was
standing next to him and he felt her hand touch his back and slowly
work its way up, and back down. He looked at her, embraced her and
passionately kissed her.

When Mark started heading for home it was almost five in the
morning. He arrived back at his apartment on United Street. The
furniture was entirely different, however. The apartment was largely
the same as it remained to be in the Twenty-First Century, even with
the refrigerator, stove, and fixtures being different. He reached in his
pocket and put the change on the nightstand next to the bed. He hung
his shirt in the closet on metal hangers and draped his pants on the
chair next to the bed, as he'd always done.

As he climbed into bed, he thought to himself, "What a weird dream
I'm having." All of this was unlike anything else he'd ever

experienced. It was all so real, and the timing was so accurate. Plus, he could smell things like the cigarette smoke at The Victoria Restaurant, the musky atmosphere at The Blind Pig/Sloppy Joe's and Glades' French perfume. Then again, the sensations of making love to Glades were so real. However, he was very tired. Sleep came quickly, in only a matter of seconds.

The alarm went off on his iPhone at nine o'clock, as always. He reached over, grabbed it, looked at it, and then turned off the alarm. He saw he had a few news notifications and other alerts from social media accounts. There were a few messages from friends and acquaintances. Checking his email, he found some interesting messages that piqued his interest. These were from firms from which he had purchased products in the past. One company wanted him to buy another vintage watch. It was an 1890 Fitz Roskopf pocket watch from Switzerland, of course. It was his style for sure, and the price was under four hundred dollars and fully mechanical, naturally from that era, as it should be.

The watch had some wear. He liked that though, so there were some scratches, wear, and tear. However, the crystal was clear and the ad said it worked perfectly. The numbers were perfectly visible and the hands appeared to be in order. The watch had his name on it as far as he was concerned.

Suddenly the pocket watch triggered his memory of Glades' brooch in the dream last night. What an odd dream it had been. He put the phone down. His interest in the pocket watch was suddenly on hold as he began to recall all of the details, the oddity of how everything seemed to be in real time. The smells of the restaurant and bar, as well as the flavor of the beer he had come back to him.

He sat up in bed, startled. He swore he smelled the perfume that Glades had been wearing. It was faint, but enough to raise a question as to whether it was real or not.

This was too weird. He jumped out of bed and bolted for the shower, not even bothering to turn on the light. The illumination from the opaque, smoked glass bathroom window would suffice. It wasn't perfect, but for that matter, the thought of turning on the light startled him. Best just jump in the shower, no questions asked, or answered. Mark didn't realize it in the moment, but the simple fact was, that he was confused and scared.

The water was cold, but he didn't care. His head was a bit foggy, though not too bad, just a touch. Funny, he didn't drink anything last night, right he thought.

When he finished, he put on his underwear and went into the kitchen to make a pot of coffee. From the kitchen window, he saw the palm trees, and someone had parked a brand new Mustang on the street outside of his apartment. "Nice," he thought and continued to gaze out the window. It was as though he'd been away and was back home, watching the world go by until he heard the coffee machine gargling the finale.

He grabbed the carafe and poured it into an old coffee cup he purchased at a yard sale. He liked old things. An old man once said to him, many years ago, "They don't make things like they used to" and he was right. Vintage items had become a quest for him over the last twenty of his nearly forty years. He often thought of the antique store he worked at back in Brooklyn with a smile and a nod, if only to himself.

His mirth accelerated when he laughed to himself, thinking of what his friend Chris would always say. "Pour it in at a forty-five-degree angle. It's the only way to do it. And for cripes sake, don't put anything in it! Drink it black. Do it any other way, and you're masking the true flavor of the particular coffee. You'll lose all of the beautiful nuances."

He adhered to the philosophy because he could see it was the true and authentic way to drink coffee as a purest. Mark certainly was a purist, as well. His appreciation of things was pure, and historic was paramount.

Mark put the coffee on the table in the kitchen and opened his back door off the kitchen. It was private, so no one could see him. A fence surrounded the property with a large hedge growing on it, secluding the yard from the rest of the neighborhood. The local paper, The Citizen, was waiting, lying on the step. He grabbed it and returned to go inside. The air was fresh and clear. with a twinge of salt. He took a few deep breaths to enjoy it. On an island over one hundred miles out to sea, this was the norm, and he never took it for granted. Key West doesn't have the pollution that cities on the mainland have. He stepped back inside. The coffee smelled fantastic. Between the fresh, clean, salt air outside and the fresh coffee brewing inside, it was a feast to his olfactory senses. The natural local scents outside, plus the man made fragrance inside, made this the start of a great day. And a great day it would be. He had the next two days off.

He read the front page of the paper, savoring his coffee more than the paper, that was certain. Nothing really all that interesting, just the usual local politics. The coffee was perfect. He usually ordered it online and kept a wide assortment from all over the world at home at all times. Today's brew was Jamaican Blue Mountain.

Mark grabbed a second cup and got some ham and eggs going on the stove. He made the eggs with slices of bread that he hollowed out a hole big enough for the yoke and fried the eggs inside the hole. He seasoned the combination with a savory sauce called Pickapeppa, add a Caribbean hot sauce to it, then sprinkle a Cuban seasoning on it called Sazon. He called it Key West eggs.

When it was done, he put them on a plate and returned to the table. He had already looked at the main pieces in the paper. Now it would be the interesting ones that he would read, the ones that truly perked his interest. This was his morning routine every day as he ate breakfast.

One section was called "The Voice." Here readers wrote in about almost any local topics, but only a few sentences. It was always entertaining. Mark always went to it first, like so many Keys readers. It was on page two. When he opened the paper, his jaw dropped.

It wasn't "The Voice" that caught his attention on this day. It was next to that, where another small piece resided called Today in Keys History. In this section, it said, "Eighty Years Ago Today" and had a picture of the Victoria Steak House.

"Holy shit!" he exclaimed out loud. Quite loudly actually. It was a small picture, but it was clearly the same place that was in his dream last night. In the photo was a man standing in front of one of the doors. Underneath it was a caption that read "Bartender Frederick ("Freddy") Wilson stands in front of The Victoria Restaurant, 201 Duval Street, 1935."

He looked closer at the picture. It was quite small, but the figure was, without a doubt, the man he worked with in last night's dream.

"What the hell is going on here?" He again exclaimed out loud to no one but himself.

He peered into the photograph for several minutes. No doubt about it, This was the same Freddy he was with in the dream last night. How could this be? Before his dream last night, he had never known of the Victoria Restaurant, and now here it was in the paper the next day!

He put the paper down. He was completely bemused by the whole thing. He sat in a trance without moving for several minutes. What was going on here?

After pondering the situation for awhile, he concluded that the only thing to do was research. It was his day off, and he had nothing scheduled anyway, so he thought he'd run off to the library.

He went back into the bedroom and pulled his pants off the chair and got a fresh shirt to wear. There was change on the nightstand, so he swept that off into his hand. It had an odd ring to it, which caught his attention. He looked at them in his hand and found two Liberty quarters, dated 1923 and 1931. A mercury dime, 1933, and a few pennies of similar vintage. His jaw dropped again. Was this the change that Skinner gave him in the dream? No. If he were to tell a psychologist about this, he'd be institutionalized. He looked again at the coins. It would be odd having just one 1930's quarter mixed in with his change, but three coins from the 1930's?

Maybe some unfortunate soul, in his last attempt to buy something to eat, spent these last coins, coins he saved for years, on a meal, or even cigarettes? There was a sizable homeless population in Key West. They arrived here and couldn't go any further. Key West was the last stop. Besides, if you were homeless, where would you rather live? Chicago, New York, Boston, Detroit, Atlanta, Washington

D.C., or Key West in October through May? The bright ones came to Key West.

It made no sense to him whatsoever. The Key West library was definitely his destination.

When Mark arrived at the library, he though to himself, "What am I doing here?" It was his day off, after all. Were there not all sorts of activities to pass the pleasure time with? Yet, here he was, entering the library, about to look up eighty-year-old local history. Interesting indeed, as vintage was a keen hobby of his, but this was certainly not up the alley he had planned for the day. At least not as of when he went to bed last night.

The doubts were overcome quickly. Everything was so real. He could still hear Glades and Freddy's voices and see their faces, as though it was... well, last night.

Going into the city records, he was amazed to find that, indeed, the current Sloppy Joe's had been the Victoria Restaurant prior to becoming Sloppy Joe's in 1937. While he already knew the famous story of the patrons leaving what is today Captain Tony's and carrying their cocktails to the newly leased Sloppy Joe's on Duval Street, he never did know the location's previous name. All he only knew was that it moved. Yet, there it was, in black and white, stating that the name was exactly the same as he knew it in the dream. He suddenly felt a bit light-headed.

How could this be? This was really weird. Too weird, actually. He sat in bewilderment, just gazing at the text for quite a long time.

After a few minutes, his mind started working. What about these people?

Mark decided to look them up via the U.S. Census. He found out that one had been conducted in 1930. Close enough, he thought.

Figuring out how to check Key West's census was easier than he expected, thanks to the internet. In 1930, Glades would have been twenty-one, he thought, and as his dream took place in 1935. She would have been twenty-six at that time.

Suddenly, there it was. Glades Yolanda Valdez. Born March 9, 1909, Key West, Florida. Daughter of Alfredo Valdez and Lourdes Ochoa de Valdez.

"What the hell is happening here, anyway?" Mark uttered out loud. The librarian heard him and came over.

"Is there something wrong?" he inquired.

Startled, Mark turned abruptly around.

"No, uh, no. I'm sorry. Something I found was just amazing!"

"No worries," said the librarian. "It happens quite often here. These islands have a very different vibe than anywhere else, I've found. Some eye opening things happen here." He smiled and walked away.

Mark continued searching and then, sure as anything, there was the name Frederick Avery Carpenter, born January 5th, 1902, to parents Stewart Avery Carpenter and Rachel Janet Curry Carpenter. It also listed several siblings.

Mark let out a long breath, this time holding back anything audible but shaking his head slowly.

What was happening here, anyway? The location that is Sloppy Joe's today, was the Victoria Restaurant in his dream that took place in 1935. Although he had never known that beforehand, that was the case in his dream.

The people, Freddy Carpenter and Glades Valdez, were people who actually existed. He could see it clearly in the census. Their birth dates corresponded with their ages. On top of that, the dream was so real. It had been in real time. Everything time-wise was exactly like in real life. Talking to Freddy and working with him was just as it was just like real life.

He was puzzled. What about that Royal Beer? After around twenty more minutes, he found that as well. He'd never heard of it before, but it was there in his dream, crown top and all.

Then there was the change that he had. He pulled it out and saw it was the exact amount left from what he paid the bartender, Skinner, at the old Sloppy Joe's. He looked up Sloppy Joe's and found that, back in the 1930's, they had a big, black, three hundred pound bartender named... you guessed it, Skinner.

In his entire 39 years, nothing was even remotely as perplexing as this quandary. He got up from his chair at the library, gathering notes taken from pages he'd printed, putting them in his satchel.

The supporting librarian passed again and in a friendly demeanor, inquired, "You've finished? Did you find everything you were looking into?"

"So far," Mark replied, "Though I'm really not sure what to make of it all, to be honest."

The Librarian smiled and shook his head "I've been in places like you are myself. Sometimes it all comes together in stages."

Of course, the librarian could never have a clue as to what he was going through, Mark thought. What could a librarian do to explain what was going on? For the first time in his life, he was thinking a shrink was more along the lines of what could help get to the bottom of this oddity.

"Thanks for your offer to help my research. I just might take you up on it next time. If there is a next time," Mark said as he shook the librarian's hand.

"It's plain to see you'll be back to see us. I'd be happy to help when that time happens. The library always holds the key to locked doors. Often, it's just a matter of applying the correct key to its mate, the lock. Have a great afternoon!"

As he left the library, Mark felt almost as though the librarian had an air of inside knowledge. But, what would he know, anyway? He was just a custodian of information housed within that library. Today, however, his help was not required.

Mark had now found all sorts of confirmation of what happened the night before, yet the answer, whatever the hell that was, remained at large.

He got on his bike and rode around the section of town known as Old Town. While his reactions to intersections, other bicyclists, cars, and pedestrians flowed on automatic pilot, his mind was delving deeper and deeper, analyzing last evening's dream, moment by moment.

He looked at his watch and saw it was 4:39. It was Happy Hour, and he was perhaps more ready than he had ever been in his life. The bike seemed to head as though it was pre-programmed to a bar where he worked, The Side Car. It was time to continue the research he started at the library, albeit this time in the form of a libation. Sauntering up the stairs of the old Victorian mansion, he headed inside to the bar.

It was empty at this point. A very beautiful, classic bar that made you feel like stories could seep out from the woodwork. A small, yet ornate glass chandelier hung from the ceiling. It had been made on the small Italian island known for its exquisite works of crystal just off Venice, Italy: Murano.

He sat down at the bar. On this shift, his friend Reese was working. They were about the same age, give or take a year. Mark ordered an Old Fashioned. Reese had a great sense of humor and, before long, he and Mark were sharing a bunch of laughs. The bar started filling up and Reese became more busy, but he always remained jovial to all. He was an excellent bartender.

At one point a friend of his, Bill, came in, a bit boisterous but good natured, as always. At the point of his second drink, he hollered across the bar, "Hey Carpenter! How about another?" Reese laughed and hollered back, "Coming up, Bill!"

Mark suddenly snapped around to Bill and said with a look that bordered somewhere between amazement and horror, "Carpenter?"

One of the quirks of Key West was that so many never know any of their friends' family names. This was, indeed, the case of Reese's family name to Mark. Interestingly enough, he'd known Reese for a few years, but in that island colloquial way, he had never known his last name.

"Yeah, Carpenter! That's him!" Bill was pointing at Reese and laughing with a roar.

Mark spun around in his chair with the speed of a detective about to ask the suspect the question that would torpedo his alibi. "Your last name is Carpenter?" His eyes were now intently on Reese.

Reese laughed, falling into the ridiculous attitude of his lifelong friend, Bill, and said, with a point of pride, "Yes sir! Reese Frederick Avery Carpenter at your service!"

Time Traveler • 4 • Reese

Reese Frederick Avery Carpenter: This was an extended English name consisting of the family names Reese and Avery, as well as what must have been an inheritance of his great grandfather's name. It could have been possibly earlier than that, for all Mark knew.

Quick on his feet in amazement, it was virtually reflex that made Mark fumble out a question that, even after he asked it, actually surprised him, especially under such unusual circumstances.

"So let me ask you. With all of these names, how do they fit together in today's world?"

It was only after he said it, he realized he had used the phrasing "in today's world."

Of course, he was in today's world. However, the phrase itself, "in today's world," was very curious, and if not to others, it was no doubt to himself. Yet it was as though he was actually believing some highly unusual situation which was a reality and had taken place.

Everyone laughed and found the statement to be funny, but it was all for different reasons than Mark did.

"You want to know how they all came about?" Reese replied, with an ear to ear grin on his face he placed his hands on the bar at a forty-five-degree angle and leaned forward to Mark.

Staying on the roll he seemed to be on, Mark declared, "Yes, indeed! Do tell!"

"Okay! Well, here we go on my family name, Carpenter. From Scotland. My ancestors arrived in the Americas in the early seventeen-hundreds, actually. During the American Revolution, they were Tories, from Connecticut."

At this point, Bill interrupted him, asking "Tories? What's that?"

"The Americans who sided with the King."

Bill's eyes widened as though he didn't have a clue such people existed, but he didn't dare open his mouth again in question and further prove himself an ignorant fool.

Sensing this, Reese interjected, "Between fifteen and twenty percent of people living in the Colonies were Tories, Bill."

Bill bobbed his head as though it was common knowledge, but in his cloaking feign, it was definitely news to him.

"You must have either been sleeping in seventh-grade history class, playing footsie with the girl sitting in front of you, or more than likely, in the principal's office!" Mark cracked.

Everyone laughed, then Reese continued.

"After the Revolution, the Carpenters left for the Bahamas, a British possession."

He paused, cocked his head and looked inquisitively at Bob, as though to say, "You do know The Bahamas were a British Territory, don't you?". Though he said nothing, the look in his eye said it all.

"Yeah, yeah, yeah, just continue with the story," Bob retorted.

Laughing, Reese continued. "They emigrated and lived in Green Turtle Cay. At some point, we think around 1830, one of their Bahamian born sons emigrated to Key West, along with about half of Green Turtle Cay. They were among the first English-speaking settlers in the Keys, specifically Key West. The Spanish only used the island as a work station for fishing. They never actually settled here. By the way, did you know that in the Bahamas, people of European descent are known as Conchs?"

That piqued the curiosity of everyone in the room. As it was, anyone born in the Florida Keys was classified as a Conch. Again, this was an education to all. Who knew that Conchs brought their nickname with them from the Bahamas when they settled throughout the Florida Keys? An education made and the connection was established. Thank you, Professor Carpenter!

"I'm actually a seventh-generation Conch!" continued Reese, his tone a distinctive with pride.

"So there you go. Now you know my background," he laughed, and Mark, Bob, and the others at the bar laughed with him.

"But surely there's more! What about the Reese, or the Avery?" asked Mark. Then with a definite different, yet insecure tone, "And what about this Frederick?" Then picking up the confidence, Mark blurted out, "What's the story on that? A hand me down name or something?"

This was all good for bar banter. Everyone was smiling, having a classic time, almost to the point that it was at Reese's expense, but as he had such a good nature it was all good fun.

"Okay, Mark, here you go if we must. The Avery and Reese are likewise Bahamian-rooted names of like Tories, whose sons and daughters emigrated to Key West. They were names of my paternal great grandmother and my maternal grandmother. Frederick was the name of my great-grandfather, who, get this..."

Then he leaned forward from behind the bar, paused for what seemed an eternity, then finally stated: "Was a bartender here in Key West!"

The bar erupted in buoyant laughter.

"It's true! Bartending must be in my genes! Yeah, he worked a few places from what I'm told. A bunch of bars that have closed over the years, and there was some restaurant apparently that was where Sloppy Joe's is today!"

Mark laughed as well. It was a well orchestrated facade, however. A chill went through his body that extended directly to his very bones.

After about a half hour, Mark left the bar, got on his bike, and rode home. Here it was, dusk and the memory of last night's dream was as fresh in his brain as several minutes ago in "The Side Car."

Time Traveler • 5 • An Alternate Reality

Mark got back to his apartment, made an easy dinner and sat down at his computer. He looked at all of his social media sites, updating himself from earlier when he looked at in in the morning. He also looked up various things of his own personal interest: music, current movie reviews, the news of the day. He buried himself in all of this to the point that when he got up to get a drink out of the refrigerator, he noticed that several hours had passed. It was at this point that he realized that being on the computer actually took him away from his dream. In realizing this, he also realized that his entire day was fixed around the dream from the night before.

Whenever he had a strange dream he would ponder it, on and off, for maybe an hour at the very most, but usually far less. However, here he had spent eighty-percent of his day researching the background of his dream, but it was still as clear as reality was, nearly twenty-four hours later.

It was a long day and thankfully, tomorrow was his second day off. Looking at the clock, he saw it was eleven-thirty. He considered going out. After all, there was always some place to go and something to do in Key West. This town has never been accused of being boring.

A few text messages had come in on his phone from friends, beckoning him to meet them at a few nearby watering holes, but he was tired. Usually, he'd turn in around one or two in the morning. He thought he'd stay in tonight, get a long sleep, in hopes of being refreshed for tomorrow.

When he got into bed, he truly realized just how tired he was, completely relaxed, and fell asleep immediately.

When he woke, it was 6:37. He headed to the bathroom feeling well rested. He was never one to sleep long hours, for the most part. Four to six hours worked well enough. He went back to bed, but now he couldn't sleep.

Getting up again, he dressed and went to sit down at his computer. Suddenly, he felt a bit dizzy. He reached for the chair, closing his eyes as his head spun. He felt as though he was swirling for, maybe fifteen seconds. When he opened his eyes, everything was different. His jaw dropped.

Was he back into the dream? Or was this real? The stove was an old gas unit, the refrigerator was an old-style ice box. The clock was also old and different, but the time was the same. He went to the window and saw a Model-T Ford parked out front. The Mustang, which he saw earlier that morning, was nowhere to be seen. Mark was perplexed, putting it mildly.

As he looked out the window, he had a realization. The last time he had been sleeping when the peculiar dream occurred. When he awoke, he was back to normal.

Right now, however, he was fully conscious. He wasn't asleep at all. There was no computer, just the chair in which he had been sitting. It actually was a different chair. He got out of the chair and walked around his room. It dawned on him that, at this point, he was either absolutely crazy or, this was some kind of an alternate reality.

He exited the front door and headed out. Walking down United Street, he noticed most of the homes were the same, yet somehow newer. They were not as ornate and colorful as the restored versions over eighty years in the future, however. There was no doubt about it at all, this was real. How was this happening? Why was it happening to him? How could he get back? With the dream, all he did was wake up. Right now he couldn't wake up because he never went to sleep to begin with.

He got to Simonton Street and looked south to the water. Was it ever different! The Reach, a modern hotel, was not there at all. Instead, there was a small beach and on it, an airy diner/bar.

He walked down to it. In the front, facing the Atlantic, there was a large screened-in porch with a sign that read "Open 7 am – 1 am". Underneath it hung another sign, which read "Breakfast." On the roof over the door was a sign: "Jack's." In his regular time, he carried a cell phone, which provided him time, plus a myriad of functions. He not yet put that in his pocket before this insane return step back into 1935. It was still charging on his nightstand back in his regular time. However, he realized he had his Roskopf pocket watch, which in his time would be vintage; here it was contemporary. He pulled it out and flipped opened the cover open. It read 7:02 am and breakfast seemed like a good idea at this point. He wished he had the phone, nonetheless. He relied on it so much in the twenty-first century. How would it fare here? Another curiosity that remained unanswered.

He opened the screen door and went in. Ceiling fans rotated slowly, while the breeze of the trade winds streamed through the restaurant. Those marvelous trade winds! Some things don't ever change throughout the years, he thought.

He walked up to the bar and sat down on the side offering a view of the water. That was the same as well and made him feel strangely at home, under the circumstances, because the Straits of Florida, part of the Atlantic Ocean, was home for this New Englander. He noticed there was one other patron at the bar and a couple sitting at a table. That was it but it wasn't surprising though as Jack's had just opened.

The cook walked up and greeted him. He was an overweight guy, a bit unkempt, smoking a cigarette out of the side of his mouth, which bounced up and down when he talked. The cigarette struck Mark as highly unusual. In his time, a chef would be fired on the spot for smoking in an eating establishment. Then again, this was nineteen thirty-five. Things are different. "When in Rome," as the saying goes. Suddenly he had an urge for a cigarette.

"Good morning and welcome to Jack's! Coffee to start?" the cook asked, handing Mark a menu.

"Perfect," replied Mark.

"What kind? American, with cream and sugar? Cuban coffee? Or a con leche?"

"How about a buchi now with a con leche chaser, to go with breakfast?" Mark answered.

"I like your style, Mac! That'll wake your ass up!"

At this point, an attractive woman, about thirty and dressed in a white waitress uniform, breezed by, tossing her right arm up in the air casually, and, with a flip to her wrist, laughed. "Don't mind Ol' Beans! He calls every one Mac! Except me, that is!"

Everyone laughed an earnest laugh.

Cuban coffee, or Cafe Cubano, in Spanish, is a type of espresso made with sugar utilized in the brewing process. A buchi is a small serving, consisting of about an ounce or two. Loosely translated, it means "a little sip". Outside of Key West, you'll see it referred to as a "cafecito." Cafe con leche translates into coffee with milk, so casually it's known as con leche. The con leche uses scalded milk, originating from Cuba. The holy trinity of coffees with milk is the Latte from Italy, the cafe au lait from France, and the cafe con leche from Cuba. Essentially all three are almost identical and revered almost on a sacramental level.

Ol' Beans went over to the Italian espresso machine and started preparing Mark's buchi. The con leche would come later.

The espresso machine was a marvel! It was actually set up to make several elixirs at a time. In addition to having several espresso machines within itself, it also had steam tubes jutting out of its side for scalding the milk. In the center, a large bronze tabernacle like water tank rose up a full two feet from the main section of the machine. Sitting on top was a majestic bronze eagle, wings spread and head cocked to the side. As far as coffee machines went, this was unquestionably true royalty.

At this stage of the coffee game, espresso machines could only be found in the Italian sections of New York City, Boston, Philadelphia, and the Cuban areas of Florida Keys, Tampa, and Miami. A large Cuban community had sprung up in Key West thanks to the cigar industry in the 1850's. They've been an integral part of the community ever since.

One can't avoid being impressed when walking into an establishment and seeing this wonder of the coffee world. It's practically religious.

Ol' Beans brought the buchi over and asked "Breakfast?"

Mark smiled, then grabbed it and downed it, like he was doing a shot of whiskey. It tasted exactly the same as it did in his own time. Ol' Beans had one for himself as well. He likewise downed his in the exact same fashion. Mark was grateful watching Ol' Beans quaff the cafe. The ritual hadn't been diluted over the years.

He then raised the menu and gazed at it briefly. Mark looked at the cook and asked, "Grits and grunts, or ham and eggs?"

Suddenly the waitress breezed in behind the counter. "I'll take the gentleman from here, Ol Beans! Thanks for starting while I was setting up!"

"She's got you from here on, Mac. Careful, she's a sassy one!" He laughed, "The grunts are right off the boat, by the way. No bones guaranteed!" He retreated to the kitchen.

Grits and grunts are a traditional Conch breakfast throughout the Florida Keys. From Key West to Key Largo it was a breakfast staple for the folks who were born there and called themselves Conchs. A grunt is a small, tropical fish, that actually does grunt when you catch them. The name is quite appropriate.

Mark thought briefly. Grits and grunts may be a traditional Keys breakfast, but in his time, the tradition was fading away, unlike the Cafe Cubano. He figured he'd go with tradition while he had the chance.

"I'll go with the grits and grunts. Can I get a couple of eggs with that?"

"Sure, how do you want your eggs, Love?"

That caught Mark off guard for a brief second. It was seldom that one in his world would greet a stranger as "Love." However, with this waitress, it seemed completely commonplace.

He smiled and took a breath after the surprise. "Uh, sunny side, please."

"Oh! You want 'em lookin' right back at you! Got it! Cuban toast or white?"

"Yeah, and Cuban toast please."

Mark looked at the silver nameplate just below her right shoulder. "Cynthia."

She smiled, finished writing Mark's breakfast down on her paper ordering tab and scurried off. Mark looked at the Atlantic. The Straits of Florida carry the tropical waters of the western Caribbean around Cuba to merge with the Gulf of Mexico. This is where the Gulf Stream begins. It then flows past Key West and picks up additional water from the Caribbean that has flowed from the east side of Cuba.

Mark always admired the fact that every day the water appeared different. Consistent inconsistency had prevailed. It's characteristics were the same here in 1935. No doubt about it: here was natural, organic beauty. Mother Nature at her finest daily improvisation. A few people wandered in. Most sat down at tables, but one tall gentleman wearing a Panama hat sat at the bar a few seats down from Mark.

"Good morning," the man with the hat said.

Mark returned the greeting, as Cynthia brought his con leche. He took a sip and then stopped, looked back at the man sitting a couple of stools from him. The Panama hat made him look somehow familiar. Who was he? He knew him from somewhere, and it was somewhere recently.

The man turned to him and smiled. He could see Mark was trying to place him as Cynthia brought his grits and grunts.

"Yesterday. Library. Librarian," the man said quietly, almost under his breath.

Mark looked at Cynthia briefly, saying thanks as she placed the breakfast in front of him, then snapped his head around to look back at the man with the Panama hat.

"I think I need to talk to you!" Mark exclaimed.

He picked up his plate and sat down right next to the man.

"You obviously know what the hell is going on here. Is this some crazy ass dream or what?"

Cynthia came back. "Oh, you know Arthur! Any friend of Arthur's is a friend of mine!"

"Ham and eggs, please, Cyndi. Let's go sunny side today and potatoes," Arthur said, giving the order with a smile.

"You're so unpredictable, Arthur!" She said, laughing. "Every time it's different!"

"Now, onto what is happening here, Mark. You are going by Mark here, aren't you?"

"Yeah, it's the only name I've ever had. So what the hell is all of this anyway? How do you know my name?"

Mark felt perplexed, irritated, wary, scared and about a dozen or so other emotions, all rolled into one.

"Eat your breakfast first. We'll leave here and have a talk someplace more private," Arthur stated bluntly, but politely.

"I need to know…" Mark started excitedly.

"Oh, I *know* you do!" Then Arthur repeated, "Eat your breakfast first. We'll leave here and have a talk someplace where we can be alone."

Arthur paid the tab and as they were walking out said, "Always be very careful you don't have something like a quarter that is minted in 2006, or anything like that. You can imagine the headaches that will entail." Mark smiled and nodded as though it was something he hadn't considered until that point.

The opened the spring-loaded screen door and passed through onto the sandy beach.

"The beach will do, I believe. Let's sit down by those coconut palm trees over there, and hope we don't get beaned with an eighty-two year old coconut!"

They both laughed as they headed to the palm grove, which consisted of eight palm trees, maybe sixty yards away.

Mark thought of a few years earlier, in his own time, the City of Key West didn't want to plant coconut palms, citing that they weren't indigenous to the area. Well, here was a small cove of them, in nineteen thirty-five no less, and they apparently have been here long enough to be twenty-five feet high.

Mark mentioned this to Arthur as they approached the palm grove.

"The City, in our time, is just loaded with bureaucratic bullshit. Amazing the things they spend their time on, isn't it?"

They sat down in the sand leaning against two palm trees, maybe six feet apart from each other.

Mark started off direct and to the point.

"Okay, so what the fuck is going on? I accept where I am, but have no clue whatsoever on how all of this shit came about. Yesterday you were in the library in Key West 2017, and now you're sitting in a palm grove with me in 1935. What the fuck is happening here?"

Arthur started off calmly. It was more than apparent that this was not his first go around with a situation of this sort. No, Arthur had done this many more times than a first timer would first assume.

"To begin with Mark, I may call you Mark?"

"Yes, of course! Please continue," Mark retorted.

"Good. To begin with, you're not in the twenty-first century, this is 1935. People here don't talk like you. You're in their house, so you need to talk like them. Using a phrase like 'What the fuck?' doesn't exist yet. People in this time period are much more polite than in your time. Erase the word fuck from your vernacular. It virtually doesn't exist here.

"My time? Okay, what is your time then? What the hell is happening here?" Mark burst out.

"In short Mark, you, like myself, are a time traveler. If I may use the phrase 'My time is your time', you and I are from the same period."

"Time traveler? What the fuck? I'm thirty-nine years old. Why hasn't this happened before… and how the hell do I get back? Time Traveler. I thought that was wild fictional stories!"

"It was fiction for both of us until it happened, wasn't it? I'm 56 and I've been time traveling for over thirty years. Since I was twenty-three, as a matter of fact. I was as bewildered as you, perhaps even more as I was younger when it happened the first time. As time and travels go on, you'll be more and more in control of it, where and when you go as well. Starting off, you'll just go someplace, like here, for instance, without warning or choice.

I'll tell you a funny one. I've been in conversations with people at the library when suddenly it's time to time travel. I'd be gone for two weeks, then come back to my own time and back to the library in the exact moment I left, completing the sentence I started!"

Mark was dumbfounded by this revelation. "Okay, how do I control it? Let's say I don't want to do this anymore?"

Arthur smiled and shook his head slowly. "You really don't have a choice at first. You'll start to feel slightly light headed. That's when it's time to release control and go. If you don't, you'll progressively feel worse and worse. Regardless of where and when you go, when you get to your destination, you'll feel as well as you've ever felt in your life. In a short time, you'll learn how to bring it on yourself, and even pick your own times and destinations."

How bizarre was this? Seriously? Time traveling? It may have been around 8 in the morning, but he felt like he could use a shot of rum or whiskey. This wasn't the average thing to digest, yet here he was, in 1935.

Arthur said nothing while Mark took it all in. Mark looked out at the surf rolling in. Small waves were rolling up to the shore, the water in various stages of blue, dark blue, and aqua blue, depending on the depth, the sunlight and the time of day. Every day the water was different and every day it was beautiful. He took a deep breath. The air here was exactly the same as his own time.

"I get the impression you've known other time travelers?" Mark inquired.

"Oh yes, many. In time, no pun intended, you will too," replied Arthur with a lilt of mirth and a sly cracked smile.

"But tell me, how does this all come about? How did I get chosen? Who controls all of this?" Mark had so many questions.

"That's a mystery to all, actually. Some of the earlier travelers say it's the choice of God. Though today they are long since departed from this world, many six or eight hundred years ago, whose, travels will cross your path on your own travels. Now other travelers will scoff at the religious connection entirely, much like religion and politics in our time. Everyone has an opinion on exactly what the phenomenon is, and no one would ever argue that it's a not a phenomenon, no one knows, other than it does happen. It's happening right now, and that's why you and I are living in 1935 at the moment."

Arthur paused, then continued, "We also have what we call hubs. These are places and times where we congregate. Key West, 1935 is one of those places. A case in point, you and I are both here right now. You will meet other travelers here in Key West as well on future visits. Around the world, there are others, in different times. You may at one point or another find yourself in London, in the 1890's. We don't know how or why this happens, only that it does. In a short time however, you will be able to control where you visit.

We're able to utilize these hubs in times and places to gather and work together, with minimal interference with the local culture. Stick with the hubs for now. It's safer."

"How will I know what, where, and when a hub is? How do I get there?" Mark inquired.

"As a new Time Traveler, it's a natural thing. We all get sent to hubs by no choice of our own. If you want me to explain that, it's a lot like why we are time travelers. We just don't know," Arthur explained.

Mark was left without an answer. Apparently, there was no answer. One of the many mysteries which would be left unanswered.

They continued talking for quite a while, then Arthur said "You have a bicycle at your house and I have mine with me. Let's take a ride. I need to show you something very important. It has to do with the two fundamental rules we, as time travelers, must adhere to."

"I have a bike at my house?" Mark was surprised.

"Yes, as a matter of fact, in this lifetime, you'll own your house outright. We'll get to that later Let's go." Arthur explained with a friendly smile.

"I will own my house?" Mark asked in a bewildered fashion. More mysteries.

"Yes, I'll explain later. You don't at the moment."

They got up, left the beach, and headed back to Mark's house. Arthur's bike was leaning on the side of the restaurant, which he walked with next to Mark back to his house. It was only about a five-minute walk and, when they arrived, Arthur pointed out that Mark's bike was in the garage.

Sure enough, there was a black, old style bike in the garage, but it looked virtually brand new. He'd love to have this bike in his time. Talk about retro! In his own time, Mark was the personification of retro.

He wheeled it out of the garage, closed the barn style doors, and inquired, "Where are we off to?"

"The graveyard," Arthur replied dryly.

They rode to the Key West Graveyard. They both knew the way, naturally, but in a town full of little side streets, there was more than one way to skin the cat, so to speak.

The Key West Graveyard was established in its current location in 1847. It is an above ground cemetery, much akin to the better known New Orleans cemeteries, and has its own individual roads, wide enough for one vehicle. Mark knew it well, and many of the graves were ones he had studied, so fascinated by this fact, the history of the city itself.

"Follow me closely," Arthur instructed as they entered into the graveyard and up one of the roads. Arthur then placed his hand on Mark's shoulder as they rode.

Things suddenly seemed peculiar again. Everything started swirling, then it was back to normal. Mark knew that time had changed again, but this time Arthur remained with him. It dawned on him that this was the first time he time traveled with someone else.

"Everything good? Welcome to 1966!" Arthur exclaimed as he took his hand off of Mark's shoulder.

"What are we doing in 1966?" Mark inquired

"I'll show you. We'll head back to 1935 when we're done here."

Arthur rolled up to a mausoleum. It was a new, majestic mausoleum, quite ornate. The roof was gabled, and in the wedge was a large nameplate which read "Fields."

"This mausoleum was finished only a year ago. It sat vacant for months, however, it did receive its first occupant a few months back, Brian Fields," Arthur announced.

Mark and Arthur hopped off their bikes. There was a locked glass door and when they looked inside, they could see the hallway with provisions for six interments, three on either side. The angle was bad, but one had a nameplate.

"This is a very important fixture for both of us, for any time traveler, actually. We have only a few rules to abide by and Brian Fields is a prime example of one of them." Arthur continued. "He was born in London, England in 1972 and died in Key West in 1966."

Mark, again, was dumbfounded. This Brian Fields was obviously a time traveler and must have died on one of his voyages.

Arthur chuckled as if reading Mark's mind. "You're on the right track, however, it's more involved than it appears.

We have two main rules when time traveling. The first is like Brian Fields. Brian time traveled to Key West, like us, to the 1930's. It's a hub, don't forget. He arrived and was enamored with the island, as so many are. However, when he went back to his own time, which is our time, by the way, he did a lot of research on how various investments would fare on the island, so he started investing in good looking businesses and properties.

The catch is, when time traveling for one's own advancement in a particular time period, one becomes cemented in the time and can no longer return to their natural time environment. It's one thing to set things up for the future. We'll get into that later. However, to set up camp for one's own profit, and live in that time period, is another story. Therefore, Brian Fields was stuck in Key West in the 1930's. Once he did that, he was stuck in a life in 1935. He became very successful, as you can see by his mausoleum. He died physically at sixty-five years old, however, in reality, he was negative six years old. You and I stand here now, in 1966 at his grave site and guess what? In six years he'll be born again and live the exact same life all over again. Then when that ends, it will repeat itself over and over. It's a life loop. He will never attain eternal rest.

It's very important that you remember this. It's your option. If you do take it however, I recommend you go on it as Brian Fields did. He had, or has, a life of luxury through wise research. Personally, I don't recommend it. It is said that your soul will never rest.

The other very, very important rule is, never, and I mean never, attempt to alter history. For example, let's take us. In a few moments, we'll head back to 1935. Now, you and I both know that in 1939 Hitler invaded Poland starting World War II. Likewise, on December 7th, the Japanese will attack Pearl Harbor. If you attempt to do anything to alter history in any way, you will vaporize immediately. I, fortunately, have never witnessed this, however, I have encountered several time travelers who have. What they told me was that it was very quick. The traveler was vapor within seconds, never to be seen again.

Additionally, this gentleman here, Brian Fields? We may one day bump into him. I don't know the ramifications if you, or myself, were to tell him the date of his demise. I shudder to think what may follow in that case. Steer clear is my advice."

It was a wild story, but what else could Mark expect? He was on the ride of his life! He paused for a moment. "Okay, so don't attempt to change history, I know the results of attempting to profit from a particular time utilizing future knowledge for personal advancement, and if I know it, never tell anyone about their future demise."

"That's the directive. Like any rules, there are exceptions. The hubs carry some exceptions, which we'll get into at a later date." Arthur reinforced.

"So who vaporizes you?" Mark questioned.

"I can only assume whoever made us time travelers, to begin with."

"And who is that?

"There are a few theories out there as how we came to be, but no one is really sure. We only know that we are." He laughed and then said, "Some have suggested that we're actually the reincarnated spirits of the Knights Templar!"

Mark laughed as well, then sarcastically blurted out, "Oh yeah! I can just see myself spearheading the Crusades!"

He paused and thought for a second, "You're the only time traveler I've ever met. Are there women time travelers as well?"

"Of course! Not as many as men, though. You'll meet them in time." replied Arthur.

Then Mark, quick as a whip, stated, "Women would rule out the Knights Templar theory then!"

"Actually, not really. Past lives/future lives have no effect on the spirit's sex in any way. That's solely biological."

"Why the Knights Templar then? How did they come up with them."

"That's logical when you stop and think about it. The Knights Templar were a very loyal and noble group. They stood and lived by their word of honor as well as their convictions. Their word was their commitment and their bond. Their primary objective was to protect people, and as a fighting force, they were the equivalent of today's Special Forces. If you look at it from that angle, keeping in mind that time travelers share those same exact traits, the piece fits that part of the puzzle."

Arthur mentioned he had a few affairs to attend to, but first they had to get back to 1935. He instructed Mark to follow him closely on his bike, Arthur put his hand on Mark's shoulder and suddenly, just like before, things started swirling and becoming blurry. Then it was clear again and Arthur stopped his bike and Mark followed suit.

"Okay! You're back in '35! I'll catch you a little later." They shook hands and he pedaled away.

Mark looked around the graveyard again before he left. He headed out the Margaret St. exit and saw the school on the corner of Southard Street, bustling with children at recess. This was an odd sight for him indeed. He'd lived in Key West for five years at this point, and his estimate was that, in his own time, the school had been closed for at least twenty years. It was shuttered up and the grass was often a foot high before anyone cut it. Rumor has it that an eccentric millionaire owns the property and that it's been on the market for some time. That was over eighty years in the future, yet here it was in its heyday, a thriving school.

The rest of the neighborhood looked quite similar, albeit not as colorful or restored. He continued down to the docks. Now here it was *different!* The docks were loaded with commercial fishing and shrimp boats. In his time, it was pretty much a luxury harbor, but this was a working dock. The raw bar was there, just smaller. The shrimp boat wheelhouse part wasn't there yet. He figured it was still on a shrimp boat.

It was early afternoon and he was a bit hungry. He parked his bike and went inside. Interestingly enough, the joint looked pretty similar to the place he knew over eighty years in the future with dark wood and earthy smell. The bar was the same, save for the beer taps he knew. Here there were only two, and both were the same. Right on the beer pull handle was the name "Royal". He hopped on a bar stool with a grin. He was starting to relax and enjoy this time traveling thing.

Just as the bartender approached, he felt a hand on his shoulder and a woman's voice, a bit out of breath, say "Hey Mark!" It was Glades from The Victoria Restaurant. His wonderful liaison on his last trip came to mind immediately. He liked Glades, she had a great vibe to her.

"I saw you cross Caroline Street as I left my apartment." Her apartment was a block up the street on the corner of Caroline and Fishbone Lane. It still amazed him that, many years later, Fishbone Lane would be renamed Peacon Lane. He liked Fishbone better.

She was grinning ear to ear today, dressed casually in a white button down blouse and what, in later times, would be referred to as cargo pants.

"We're both off today!" she exclaimed as she sat down next to him at the bar.

"So what do you want?" The bartender inquired. He was a pudgy guy, mid-forties, bald and a bit disheveled.

Glades didn't hesitate. " A couple of Royals and a menu, Frank."

"Okay, good. His name is Frank," Mark thought since Frank didn't have a name tag.

"Menu? You're talking to the menu!" Frank proclaimed in a loud voice followed with a hearty laugh. "We got oysters on the half shell, steamed clams, burgers, Cuban sandwich, and dolphin sandwich."

To this day, natives in the Florida Keys call the fish "Dolphin," or sometimes by its Spanish name, Dorado. Technically, the fish's English name is Dolphinfish, in order to differentiate it from the mammal with the same name, but, everyone here just calls it dolphin.

"Quiero un sandwich dorado, Francisco!" Glades blurted out in Spanglish, laughing.

"Make it two, Frank," Mark piped in quickly.

Mark found Glades fun. They had a great while enjoying the view of the water from the bar. When they finished, Glades excitedly said "Oh! I want to show you something at my place!" She grabbed his hand and rapidly led him out the open door.

Arriving at her apartment, the door closed and she wrapped her arms around him. Before long, they were together, naked, in bed again.

Glades was adventurous, which surprised Mark. He had this vision of women of the era to be seeing sex as a chore. This certainly wasn't the case with Glades. She wanted all different positions and was loud when she climaxed.

They spent around an hour or so there. After a while, Mark mentioned that he had some things to do at his house. He went back to the restaurant, picked up his bike, and pedaled back up William Street.

Suddenly, there was Arthur heading up Fleming Street. He waved as he approached riding parallel to Mark. "Let me show you a trick! You're going to need this."

"What's that?" Mark asked with a smile.

"Take a full, deep breath, close your eyes briefly, and think the words 'back to my original time'."

A bit hesitant, but with a smirk on his face, he said apprehensively "Okay."

Doing as instructed, once again he became a bit dizzy for a second and everything started swirling as they rode down the street. After about ten seconds, everything was back to normal, and Arthur and Mark were approaching the old, abandoned school on the corner of Southard and William Streets. They were back in their own time.

"Is that all there is to it?" Mark asked as they rode down the street.

"That's it. But realize, I went with you because I am right next to you. Plus, we're both time travelers. If I were not, I would see you disappear into thin air. A non-traveler can only travel with you if there is physical contact between you. I put my hand on your shoulder to demonstrate this to you, but between two travelers, it's not necessary. Within six feet or so works. In a bit, I'll show you how to come back to the exact moment you left. Get a feel for it, but when you travel, do it in seclusion for now."

"I have a few things to attend to at the library. By the way, I'm your sponsor. We'll get into that later. You mentioned in our 1935 breakfast that today is your day off. Enjoy it. I'll catch up with you soon… or before, in 1935! That is your current go-to spot, and I see you spending some time there. It's also a hub. It'll be good for you, a fabulous place to start!"

Mark pulled out his watch. He really loved his old pocket Roskopf timepiece. If it was vintage and quality, it fit his style. The Roskopf was both. It read 4:38 in the afternoon as he rode down the street. Eight minutes later he rolled into his front yard,

What a day he thought. Who could have had such a day? Seriously! Breakfast and lunch in 1935. I have a girlfriend, and I'm getting laid over eighty years ago. He laughed to himself thinking that he had a vintage girlfriend and really liked her, too.

To think that only last week hearing someone telling this tale would evoke memories of a nutty science fiction movie. Yet, here I go, time traveling back to 1935 where I have a job that pays thirty-two cents an hour and a beer costs five cents. Today a beer *starts* at five dollars!

Going out with Glades in 1935 worked well. In his current time, he didn't currently have a girlfriend. If he stuck with Glades in '35, that certainly wouldn't change. Mark wasn't the type to run around with two girls at the same time anyway, even if they would be over eighty years apart in time.

He felt he had to talk to someone about this so he called his buddy Blackheart. His real name wasn't Blackheart, of course, but the Key West tradition of having nicknames was just another piece of the town's light hearted puzzle.

When Mark first landed on the island, he worked for a while on one of the sunset sail boats as a deckhand. It was only for a few months before he landed a job bartending. While he was on the boat he met and became good friends with Blackheart.

Blackheart was the captain, and Mark, having grown up on sailboats in New York and New England, had been hired as the first mate. He knew the lay of the land when it came to things nautical. Both men spoke the same language and they worked together like a well-oiled machine.

After securing the boat after a sail, the two would often head to one of several watering holes and shoot the breeze about everything, from the sail they were just on, to the beer they were drinking, to various ports of call throughout New York and New England.

Blackheart was a fine seaman, having cut his teeth in Mystic, a truly classic New England seaport. He lived on his sailboat in Key West Bight with his charming girlfriend Sieg, as she was known, and their dog Chuck.

When Mark called Blackheart he was already getting things ready for the evening sunset sail. They spoke briefly, but Mark's tone made it apparent to Blackheart that meeting him after his sail was something that wasn't a casual "let's go out for a beer" call. There was something more to this. This was important.

They met at 8:30 that evening at The Cork and Stogie, a small, quaint bar at the quiet end of Duval Street on the 1200 block, with a marvelous beer selection.

Mark suggested sitting in the second room just off the bar, and Blackheart began to eye him warily, as if he could sense that this was something with some gravity to it.

They had Dusty, the bartender, pour a couple of craft drafts. Blackheart had a Bell's Porter, Mark an MIA Mega Mix.

"This is going to be wild, and I know you'll either think that I'm pulling your leg or that I've completely lost my mind. For the record, this is the first beer I've had today… well, kind of."

"What do you mean 'kind of'? Either you had one, or you didn't", laughed Blackheart.

Mark replied slowly, with his head tilting to the side, his voice lilting into a."Welllllll, it's a little of both actually."

"You're not making sense. Okay, I'm ready. Solve the mystery for me and explain please?" asked Blackheart with a wry awkward smile, a look, and a nod.

"This *doesn't* make any sense whatsoever. Absolutely none! But it's real. Trust me, it's real," Mark blurted out excitedly. "All I ask is that you allow me to tell you everything from start to finish. Just sit here and listen. At the end you are welcome to ask me anything or laugh at everything, just hear me out, okay?"

Over the next forty-five minutes and two more beers, Mark, often speaking in hushed, tones, explained the peculiar events of the past couple of days.

"And so, as of 4:30, I've been back on current time." With a sigh, Mark glanced at Blackheart expectantly, then looked away. In his mind, he knew at this stage how far fetched it must have sounded.

Blackheart sat back and stroked his chin. After a moment, he smiled and clapped Mark on the back enthusiastically "Well, I didn't realize you were working on a play! Is it going to be at The Red Barn? Or maybe a movie?"

"Blackheart. I'm serious," Mark said

"Of course you're serious! Now that's a plot line that should go over well in these times. No pun intended!" He laughed heartily at his own joke.

"Let's have another beer Blackheart. I'll try this call again another time."

It dawned on him that the story was so outlandish that no one would possibly believe him. He would need evidence. He couldn't blame Blackheart either If their roles were reversed, he'd be saying the same thing.

Blackheart was thoroughly teasing him while they polished off their beers.

"Hey! Let's go back to 1935 and meet at this Victoria Restaurant! You know I have to meet this Glades! What do we do, slip there via a black hole or something like that?"

Mark just looked at him, realizing that if he tried to explain any further, he might be a candidate for the DePoo Medical Center psychiatric ward across town. No, he needed something more concrete for Blackheart to take him more seriously. He realized it was so far-fetched. Definitely, here he was trying to convince people that he was time traveling when he was having a bit of a time believing it himself. He changed the subject and they talked about all sorts of things that evening, finishing up at eleven, with a six beer buzz going.

They parted ways that evening at the foot of the stairs of The Cork and Stogie and shook hands. Blackheart said wink and a smirk, "Keep up the work on that screenplay of yours, Bubba!"

Mark nodded and smiled, but as he unlocked his bike, a plan formed in his imagination. Could it work? It would have to wait until his next voyage to 1935. For now however, he was tired, very tired and he had work tomorrow. At least his shift started at 10:30 in the morning and not earlier.

He rode his bike home. It was a quick ride from the Cork and Stogie, less than five minutes. It truly had been a very long day indeed, both in 1935 and his current time.

His head hit the pillow and his lights were out. He woke up at 8:12. He slept well and he felt fully refreshed.

Time Traveling • 10 • Oh The Humanity

Mark sprung out of bed, opening the door, admiring a day which presented itself bathed in sunshine. The backyard was lush and full of colors in the tropical morning showcase. A few coconut palms to his left reached skyward, while next to them was a cluster of tall banana trees. A bougainvillea was in the corner, then to the right were another group of palms, all of which provided shade to the yard. Off to the right side was a charcoal Bar-B-Que grill. Indeed it was a tropical showcase.

It was late autumn, so the temperature was in the seventies in the morning, low eighties in the mid-afternoon. Right now it was seventy- four. He took in a deep breath as he walked back into his apartment, leaving the door open. After all, what's better than fresh air? Fresh island air! It was so invigorating.

Today, he'd be back at the bar. His shift started at ten-thirty and ended at six thirty, so he still had some quality home time left before heading in. He fired up his Braun espresso maker and proceeded to fix himself a con leche.

Throwing on a t-shirt and shorts, he headed out to the backyard to enjoy the coffee. It was the type of morning to live for! A gentle breeze moved through the palms and bougainvilleas. The sky was blue as could be with puffy clouds scattered about. He had a small, round table in the shade of the bananas and the palms where he sat staring off into space.

A blank mind never lasted long, however. He drifted off, back to 1935 and specifically, Glades. He really was attracted to this girl. He stopped and thought about it. She was, what, mid-twenties in 1935?

Here he was, over eighty years later, back in his own time. She was long gone this point, but the weird thing was, when he went back to '35, there she was, young and fresh as the day in his backyard was this morning!

Sure, Arthur was an invaluable help, he could assist in so many aspects of this time traveling, and was a new acquaintance. Blackheart was a true, trusted, dyed-in-the-wool friend, but how could he convince him that this wasn't a tall tale? As he sipped his cafe con leche in the backyard, he pondered what to do.

It all came back down to finding proof that a non-traveler would, or could, believe. In his previous travels, he never brought his iPhone with him. The first time he just went to bed and, next thing he knows, he's tending bar at The Victoria Restaurant! The second time was similar in that it was, again, something unexpected. In both cases, it happened suddenly. Disappointing as it may have been, it would be chalked up to circumstance. No preparation could have possibly been made.

This next time would be different. Now that he had a basic understanding of how to travel, things could be prepared for, something which he couldn't do before. It had been by chance that he traveled the first two times previously. The next trip would be planned and he'd take his iPhone. While it may not work as a phone in 1935, so long as long as it had a charge, why couldn't it work as a camera?

He got up and went into his bedroom. There was his iPhone on the night stand, plugged in and fully charged. He was ready and he pushed the button; the screen came on with news headlines, and a text message from Blackheart that read, "Rest well."

He didn't question the meaning between the lines. It had a bit of a sting to it, but also carried a bit of inspiration and motivation to at least give this a shot.

Opening up the phone's apps, he scrolled through the morning updates quickly. Then, realizing that he really should get the ball rolling, he started to prepare for the change back to the same date in 1935.

He put the phone in his pocket, closed his eyes, and concentrated on going back. Again, the room started spinning and after a few moments, he opened his eyes and the room was set in 1935 decor.

He looked at the Seth Thomas clock on the night stand. It read 9:06. Reaching into his pocket he pulled out his iPhone. There was the time, 9:06, but the date certainly caught his attention. December 7th, 1935. It surely amazed him that the phone was actually programed so that it would go to a date prior to its production. There it was, however.

His curiosity sparked, so he went to some other apps to find everything blank. No weather. No news. Just blank pages. He opened up his photographs and they were still there.

He then checked his camera, taking a picture of his stove; it worked well. Excellent! This is what he had hoped for!

He started photographing his apartment: the sink, the refrigerator, the room itself, the bathroom, and then the backyard. The 1935 back yard was substantially different than the backyard in his own time. There wasn't nearly as much foliage, the table and chairs were gone, a full sized wooden picnic table there instead, filling the space, and a large mahogany tree stood where the coconut palms should be.

He photographed his bike before mounting it and heading out. It was time to go someplace new; at least someplace new in that he'd never been to the 1935 edition of Key West. First stop was The Southernmost Point.

It wasn't much like the Southernmost Point of the twenty-first century time. For one thing, the buoy wasn't there. There were several African Americans selling conch meat as well as the shells. Two men were out in the water collecting them. Interesting, Mark thought. In his time, conch was regulated and illegal to harvest. However, here he was in 1935 and all business as usual, as far as conch harvesting and sales were concerned.

He took a few pictures from across the narrow street. The people there looked at him with funny expressions. One asked, "Hey, what is that thing? What are you doing?"

"Oh! It's just a camera," Mark replied.

"Camera? Where's the stand and the hood and the tripod?"

Mark laughed and waved as he rode away. "It's from the future!" he called out over his shoulder.

"Mother Mary and Joseph! Did you hear what that man said?" said another man quite loudly to his friend. Mark could hear them talking as he headed up Whitehead Street.

After a few blocks, he found himself a bit puzzled. He had just passed the old stone church on the corner of Julia. It was an active AME church. He only knew it as a church converted into an art gallery and apartment, once rented by a friend. Up ahead he saw the lighthouse, standing tall and proud. Here was the sentry of the sea standing at attention, with a beacon set to shine and ward off ships from running aground. It was set a good quarter-mile up the road from the Southernmost Point, replacing the original, which was destroyed in the hurricane of 1846.

This was not the first lighthouse. That had originally stood at the Southernmost Point and was susceptible to the hurricane which destroyed it. This is why they built the second one up the street. The new location offered a sixteen-foot elevation at the base. This has proved a sage move over the years. The lighthouse still stands proudly in Mark's time.

As he approached, he noticed that he was crossing Division Street. At this point he realized that it was 1935, and would be another ten years before President Franklin Delano Roosevelt would pass away in office, making Vice-President Truman president. Then, another three years would pass before the street would be renamed in his honor, Truman Avenue. He snapped a picture of the street sign with the lighthouse in the background.

Across from the lighthouse, a major landmark was missing. There was Hemingway's house alright, but there was no wall. It wouldn't be another two years before the red, rickety wall would be built! Mark found that truly amazing. No wall at Hemingway's house. As he pedaled by the lawn he saw a slim, dark-haired woman in her mid-thirties playing with a couple of toddlers. That has to be Pauline he thought. Another woman came out as well, causing him to stop immediately. He pulled his camera out and started taking pictures, Some he took were closeups, which he felt were imperative. Additionally, he experimented with a full panorama.

He switched the iPhone to video, then started filming. Again, he zoomed in. He had a few short recordings, the longest being maybe a minute long, the others around forty-five seconds or so. He put the phone back in his pocket.

When he looked back up, the woman, whom he figured was Pauline, was jogging over to him "Are you okay?"

Mark was taken aback for a moment. "Am I okay? Well, yes. I'm fine actually. Why do you ask?"

"I saw you rubbing your eyes with what looked a black cloth, or something. I thought you may have gotten something in your eye."

"Oh! That was nothing really. Just a small piece of dust I think." He regrouped much quicker this time. With the men at the Southernmost point, he had been rather at a loss of words for an instant, as he was put on the spot. This time he was better prepared. "Thank you for your concern! My name is Mark." He extended his hand.

She smiled and shook his hand politely. "My name is Pauline Hemingway." She was a slender, attractive woman, with short, dark brown hair.

He somehow contained his composure and thought, "Holy shit *this is Pauline Hemingway!*"

"I think I've seen you somewhere around town, haven't I?" she enquired.

"Well, I bartend at The Victoria Restaurant, perhaps that's where?" He didn't miss a beat this time. Maybe he was getting the hang of this time travel thing.

"A couple of nights ago! Yes, that's it. I saw you making drinks there! You work with another bartender as well. You made me a Manhattan. Glades was our waitress. I was watching from the table when she gave you our order. We were a group with my husband, Joseph Russell, and the Thompsons." Then she gave a little laugh and said, "It was a perfect Manhattan!"

Thank God he didn't blow that. There again, being an accomplished and well-versed bartender, he never blew a drink. Frankly, he hadn't had a moment to look at the crowd that evening. No doubt, if he made drinks for Pauline Hemingway, he also had made some for Ernest Hemingway. Perhaps it was a blessing that he didn't know it at the time.

Candidly, it just doesn't get any higher of an honor than making Ernest Hemingway a drink. Who could you make a drink for of higher esteem than Ernest Hemingway? It's an entire double play. First off, Hemingway could very well be America's greatest author. Mark was one who was of said opinion. Second, what other figure was known for his drinking and high living at bars from Key West to Barcelona to Havana? Hemingway made the bar his home away from home. Ernest Hemingway is a double dose of alcohol hierarchy! *The most royal of the royal!*

He had served his highest esteemed author and most world-renowned drinker of all time. Mark had made Ernest Hemingway a drink a few days ago... and never knew it!

"Oh, the humanity!" echoed in his mind at the thought of mixing an elixir for Ernest Hemingway. Yet, no sooner than that phrase flew through his brain than he realized the source of the saying. Herb Morrison wouldn't say it for another year-and-a-half when the Hindenburg would explode in Lakehurst, N.J. in May of 1937. It certainly was appropriate today, however. No common curse words carried the gravity of the statement to relay trauma. He served Hemingway and never knew it! Yes indeed! *"Oh, the humanity!"* It was the modern day equivalent of throwing a football with the Super Bowl winning quarterback. Driving a lap with a four-time Indy 500 champion. Stepping into the ring to spar with Muhammad Ali. Making a drink for Ernest Hemingway was that and so much more.

All of this flew through his consciousness in a millisecond. Dazed for an instant, he mumbled aloud, but not much louder than a breath *"Oh, the humanity!"*

Pauline picked up on it, however, "Oh the humanity? I've never heard that expression. What do you mean?"

Mark gathered himself up quickly. "Oh! It's a phrase my uncle said. He picked up from a fellow doughboy he was with in the last war, the battle in Verdun." He actually impressed himself with that one, which he had clearly pulled out of his ass. Then, before Pauline could reply, he chimed in, "I'm glad everything was satisfactory with your cocktails!" followed with a beaming, ear-to-ear grin.

She smiled in return "They were excellent, thank you. Now I have to get back to Patrick and Gregory, my sons. Very nice to meet you, Mark! I'm sure we'll see you again. Excuse me."

"Nice to meet you, Mrs. Hemingway," he replied.

She hadn't quite fully turned around to walk back, but she smiled again, shyly, then nodded in acknowledgment. Mark saw her pause a moment, brow furrowed. Had she mentioned her last name? No, she purposely omitted her last name when she introduced herself as Pauline. Mark impressed her as someone who was among the educated in the community. Pauline smiled to herself.

She strolled slowly across her lawn, back to her children, while Mark continued his ride down Whitehead Street. He kept saying to himself as he pondered serving Hemingway without knowledge of doing so, *"Oh, the humanity!"*

Mark arrived at the intersection of Southard and Whitehead and looked west. A block down on Thomas and Whitehead, there was a gated entrance to the Mole Pier, later sections of it would be known as The Truman Waterfront. Without proper authorization, the naval base was restricted. Mark went down nevertheless and took a few pictures of the gated entrance and the white uniform enlisted SP sailors assigned there. Where would they be in six years time when Pearl Harbor would be attacked?

He checked the time and it was now 10:12 am, 1935. He turned around and started back up Southard to Whitehead. Mark closed his eyes and concentrated on drifting back to his original time. When he opened his eyes, the current Green Parrot was just up the street and he was on his current bike. How did this all happen? Ninety-five percent of it was still a mystery.

Nonetheless, he didn't have time to ponder it now. He was off to work at The Side Car.

A thriving business could be had in Key West. Cruise ships were making Key West their port of call for the day. None stayed overnight. They'd come in for three to five hours before sailing off to their next destination: Cozumel, Freeport, Grand Cayman, or some other Caribbean port. Today would be a busy one; there were three ships scheduled in port.

Mark arrived and the bar was left in perfect order. Some bartenders would slack off and leave some chores for the morning shift. He figured it was Reese, a bartender after his own heart.

Good thing, too. The first ship had arrived and disembarked at ten in the morning. The passengers were canvassing the main drag, Duval Street, like ants already. On a four mile by mile and a half island, there are three hundred and sixty liquor licenses. Most of them are on the western part of the island, on or around Duval Street. That's not including the beer and wine licensed bars either. Who knows how many of those are here?

According to an Anheuser-Busch study, Key West has the highest alcohol consumption per capita in the United States, by a *long* shot. The main industry in Key West is not fishing or sunset sails. It's alcohol.

When Mark opened up The Side Car, it filled up within twenty minutes. The Side Car is a small, posh bar in a classic Victorian house known as The Captain Everleigh Mansion. Were it in England, it would be a "Saloon Bar."

On his shift, Mark would wear a bow tie. Ties, in general, are deeply frowned upon in Key West, some jokingly say that one might just get arrested for wearing one. A bow tie anywhere other than The Side Car, might very well get you lynched. (Key West prides itself on being casual.)

The Side Car is one of the very few high-end bars in Key West, outside of the hotel bars and Mark liked to look the part when he made his craft cocktails. Making these drinks can be time-consuming. They are quality drinks and naturally expensive. So why not give his guests the full experience?

The first ship to dock in was one of the Mardi Gras line, known for focusing on the lower budget clientele. The bartenders refer to it as

The Greyhound of the Seas, after the bus company. The people off of these boats, more often than not, are looking for frozen drinks with little umbrellas. Some will seek any opportunity to complain about prices and stiff the bartender on the tip. Mind, that's some, certainly not all. However, it's the squeaky wheel syndrome.

The usual was expected and received when the cruisers filed in off the Mardi Gras ship. Tips were around twenty percent down from average, but it was a good atmosphere, plus there were two more ships arriving shortly.

One would be The Royal Viking, around an hour and a half after the Mardi Gras liner docked. These folks were almost always high-end clientele, and they had tip money to prove it. Their tips ended up being right on the mark. The other cruise line in was the World Cruise, which did indeed cruise the world, stopping at various ports of call, from New York to Rio, to Key West, to Singapore. In addition, it is run like a timeshare. Someone might buy a cabin for a year, at one million bucks, or enjoy their aquatic timeshare from month to month.

When these folks come to town, which isn't often, it's a good day for everyone: the passengers, the vendors, the bars, and restaurants. A few wandered into The Side Car around three in the afternoon. The Mardi Gras ship left at two-thirty, so, at this point, it was all high-end clientele. Mark couldn't help but stop and wonder when orders came through periodically for the Hemingway Daiquiri. He was hoping, at his other job, the one in 1935 at The Victoria Restaurant, he'd get to mix another for Ernest himself, knowing that he was making for the literary and imbiber extraordinaire.

It was a good day, the tip jar was stuffed to the brim, mostly with tens, twenties, and even several fifties. Some kind drunk left a hundred dollar bill, as well. People, in general, were more generous when they were on vacation.

Mark's shift ended at six thirty after all the ships had disembarked for the day. It was a very prosperous day. On his way home, he stopped at the bank and deposited over seven hundred dollars. Damn good shift!

It had been a busy day, and while it had paid off big time, Mark was exhausted. He rode directly home and immediately stretched out on his bed. It was 6:54 when he looked at his clock.

He fell into a long, deep sleep, despite his intent to just take a load off for a few minutes. As it turned out, when he woke up, it was 10:30, he had slept for three and a half hours.

Turning on the lamp, he suddenly remembered his iPhone. With such a busy and draining day, he almost forgot it. But memory is a lot like fragments from a hand grenade, it lands in one space and something thirty feet away gets hit. Often something completely unrelated brings it to the surface. In this case, the lamp triggered his memory of the phone still in his pocket.

He opened the pictures app and, sure enough, there they were as clear as day. However, seeing them in the iPhone screen wasn't good enough; he had to see them on a larger screen.

Across the room, he hustled, opening up the laptop on his desk to download the pictures.

Now that the images where there and over seventeen inches wide, something caught him completely off guard. He was looking at forty-three crystal-clear pictures from 1935, taken from a twenty-first-century digital camera. This was the only place on earth that pictures like this could be found.

The only way to describe it was "off the wall." Back in the thirties, color photography was in its embryonic and infancy stages. Here were crystal clear digital pictures of Key West, circa 1935!

He decided to save the pictures in his phone even though he was downloading them to his laptop. Once they were completely in the computer, he called Blackheart.

"Blackheart! You have to come over to my place right now!" Mark barked into the phone when Blackheart answered. He couldn't restrain his excitement.

"What the hell, Brother? It's 10:40 at night!" Blackheart moaned, then adding with lightheartedness "It's not like you're Gisele Bundchen, calling me and asking me to stop by her place for a nightcap."

"Yeah, yeah, yeah, where the hell are you?" Mark anxiously inquired.

"I'm at The Flaming Anus drinking a Jai Alai IPA."

The Flaming Anus. Only in Key West. On the two hundred block of Duval Street, the wild end. When the bar was being set to open, the city stepped in because the name just was too profane to be allowed. The owners, a group of five former pro football players, had big pockets, hired a high powered lawyer, took it to the highest court in the State of Florida, and won. The argument was that there was nothing profane about it, when used an anatomical name. Had it been "The Flaming Asshole" it wouldn't have ever gotten up to bat, so to speak. To the reluctance of both City and State officials, the former football players won and "The Flaming Anus" opened for business.

It was a boisterous environment, as one would tend to expect in a place called The Flaming Anus. Mark could hear all of the commotions in the background on the phone. It was actually very difficult to hear Blackheart at all.

"Look! This is important. Come over!" Mark barked again loudly so Blackheart would hear.

"What? Hard to hear in here!" hollered Blackheart back.

"Come over! It's important!"

"Oh jeez, okay, let me finish my beer. I'll be there in about a half hour," Blackheart finally conceded.

Mark breathed a sigh of relief. Finally, he'd be able to share this with Blackheart and he knew it would take a big load off his shoulders.

A knock on the door was followed by Blackheart walking in briskly and proclaiming aloud, "It was a hell of a night at The Flaming Anus!" Of course, it was. How could it not be?

"I have no clue why you, or anyone else, go to that place. It's a miserable shithole if there ever was one," Mark said laughing as he shook Blackheart's hand. Blackheart laughed as well. That type of put down was the type that only that two real friends could both laugh at together. Still laughing, he lead Blackheart to his computer.

"Have a seat, I want to show you something," Mark said, pointing to a seat next to him. Blackheart shrugged his shoulders, nodded, then sat down saying "Okay pal, what's so important?"

Mark wiggled the mouse and the screen lit up. He went to the picture section and accessed the folder he made earlier.

"Okay, Blackheart, buckle your seatbelts."

"What are you going to show me?" Blackheart inquired.

"Hang on. Check these out," Mark said as he opened the folder and went through the series of pictures. First, there was the old bicycle. Then the backyard.

"Looks a lot like your backyard, but way different!"

Mark said nothing, only continued clicking. Next were the pictures of the folks at the Southernmost Point, selling and gathering conch.

"They can't go after conch! It's a protected species. There's a five-hundred dollar fine per conch harvested!" He was actually outraged, although still a little tipsy, from his stint at The Flaming Anus.

"Wait, there's more," Mark replied.

Next was the Division Street sign with the lighthouse in the background.

"There's the lighthouse, but what's this Division Street? What's Division Street? I smell Photoshop here?" a puzzled Blackheart asked.

"No. No Photoshop, Blackheart. Division Street was the name of Truman Avenue in 1935, Don't forget, Truman wasn't president for another ten years. Now, check this out," Mark replied as he clicked the mouse again.

The next picture was one of Pauline. It was one that he had zoomed in on. Then next was another from afar.

"Know her?" Mark asked. He then immediately left the folder and went to the internet, where he had a page open on Hemingway's history ready and waiting with a picture of Pauline. He opened it up, enlarged it slightly before flipping back to his own pictures. Back to the internet picture, and back to his.

"That's Pauline Hemingway! How did you get such a great picture of her? It looks like it was taken today. It's not an old picture." Blackheart inquired.

76

"I took it this morning. Notice anything else?" It was a leading question that Mark had proposed, and Blackheart knew the answer as soon as he looked at the picture taken from the street.

"This morning? What the...? Okay! I get you! Where's the wall?" Blackheart asked. He was in amazement at this point.

"The wall was built in 1937. This is 1935."

Mark then put on the videos of Pauline playing with her two sons. You could hear her and the kids quite clearly.

In the last video, Pauline had just started running over to Mark when the video cut out.

"How did this all happen? It looks so real!" Blackheart exclaimed.

"Blackheart, it *is* real. I had no idea how it happened at first. Honestly, I have no idea *still* how it happens, but I've been time traveling a few times now, only over the last few days. The first ones I had no control over. They just happened. No warning. It just happened. I met this guy. Let me leave his name out of it for now, but he's been doing it a lot longer than I have and he's given me some great advice and taught me as well. He's actually my mentor if you can digest that."

"These pictures are amazing. But time traveling? That's just too weird to believe, Mark. You've got a good leg pull going here, I'll give you that!" Blackheart laughed as he reached out to shake Mark's hand.

Here was the opportunity Mark had been waiting for. He laughed as well, then reached out to shake Blackheart's hand. As they shook, Mark closed his eyes and concentrated on that same day and time, in 1935.

"Waugh! What's happening? I'm feeling dizzy all of the sudden," Blackheart moaned in a puzzled state.

The next moment they were both in Mark's apartment, circa 1935.

It was his first jump where he took someone with him. For this voyage Mark now had a Wing Man.

"What the hell! What just happened to your apartment? The walls are the same, but that's it! The furniture and plumbing are different, what the hell…"

"Look out the front window," Mark instructed to his bewildered friend. Blackheart apprehensively looked out.

"Look at the streetlights, Blackheart. They're all wooden poles, not concrete."

Blackheart's jaw dropped. Out front, an early thirties Packard drove down the road, while a Model A Ford coughed, burped, backfired, and smoked down United Street.

"Is this really happening, Mark? How can it be? How do we get back?" A very bemused and puzzled Blackheart stood before him in awe.

"Yes, it's really happening. I don't know how, or why, for that matter. And yes, I can get us back." Mark replied in a reassuring, confident tone.

"This is so weird! I can't believe it! Can we go somewhere? I want to see this place!" Blackheart exclaimed. From incredulous to a kid in a candy store, Blackheart's excitement was becoming contagious, but Mark knew he had to share what, albeit little he actually knew.

"Here's the thing. Right now it's 11:45 at night and it's December 14th. The year is 1935, but if we were to travel back to our own time, it would also be 11:45 and December 14th. I have a feeling that there's a way to change that, but I don't know it yet.

"I have to work in the morning, so I need a good rest tonight. We can go out, but I want to be back in less than an hour."

"Agreed!" Blackheart eagerly blurted out.

They set out immediately, heading down South Street to Simonton Street and then left down to Jack's. The place was still open, too.

"Holy shit! Where's the Reach?" Blackheart already amazed, realizing the hotel wasn't there.

"It won't be built for another fifty, or sixty years Blackheart," Mark replied laughing "Let me buy you a beer."

The bartender was not anyone he knew from before, but hell, the only time he'd been here was for the breakfast shift when Ol' Beans and Cynthia were working.

They wandered up to the bar and sat with a view of the water, and a view like that evening couldn't be bought for any price. The waves on this particular evening were no more than two inches high and the moon was full in a clear sky. It was a most beautiful evening and scene. Through the full open front of the bar lay the beach, with the coconut palms where he'd talked with Arthur on the left. The waves were lazily lapping to the shore, while the full moon's light danced across the waves, illuminating it all.

The bartender approached asking, "What'll it be, fellas?"

Mark took the lead on this immediately "Two Royals, please". He could tell Blackheart felt more comfortable with Mark at the helm here. These weren't his waters.

He then turned to Mark and asked "What is a Royal? Is that some rum drink or something?"

"It's actually a local beer, made right here in Key West, Blackheart. For us, it's long, long gone. Nice beer though, actually. It's an all malt product."

The bartender came back with two cone-top cans of Royal. He set them on the counter and grabbed two glasses from above the bar, and pouring the cans of beer into them. Mark and Blackheart didn't waste any time in grabbing, raising, and toasting.

"To 1935!" Mark offered as he hoisted his glass.

"1935!" a still bewildered and amazed Blackheart answered as they cheered the year and each other.

There was a bit of humidity in the air, so the glasses gathered condensation quickly. The ceiling fans spun at a quick clip however, keeping the air circulating.

The bartender smiled and nodded, then said, "I haven't seen you guys here before. Is this your first time?"

Again, Mark took the lead. "First time at night actually. I've been here for breakfast with Ol' Beans and Cynthia."

The bartender laughed. "Ol' Beans! Great guy! What a character he is! Thank God I have Cynthia to keep him in line!"

Mark and the bartender laughed. Blackheart simply smiled, gathering this Ol' Beans and Cynthia were also employees.

Mark then continued, "Maybe you know Arthur?"

"Arthur? Tall guy? Always with a hat? In his fifties?"

"That sounds like him! He's the one who brought me here, to begin with," Mark replied

"Yeah. He's an interesting sort, if there ever was one, isn't he? Full of knowledge. A real intellect if I've ever seen one. By the way, my name is Jack!" stretching out his hand.

Mark and Blackheart both gave him a hand shake.

Jack was in his late forties, early fifties, about five-eight, and one-sixty. He seemed to have a perpetual smile and full of good cheer. It may have helped that it was mid-December and there was Christmas music playing in the jukebox on the other side of the bar.

The jukebox caught Blackheart's attention. He was fascinated with it. Something like this would have never been made in his own time. It was a Wurlitzer. The box, largely made out of wood, brown with a shiny varnish to it. This wasn't just a jukebox; it was a piece of art. The woodwork alone, in his time, would have cost well over two grand.

"That jukebox is gorgeous. Do you mind if I have a closer look at it, Jack? " Blackheart inquired.

"Jukebox?" asked Jack. "We call it a coin-operated phonograph. Never heard the term jukebox before, but sure! Have a look at it. It's Wurlitzer's top model. It cost an arm and a leg too! I'll have that thing forever! Just got it last May, so it's brand new! I love it! Let me show you something I did."

He came from around the bar, walking quickly with excitement, waving them both to follow. On their way, Mark leaned into Blackheart's ear. "Apparently the name 'jukebox' doesn't exist yet," he whispered. Blackheart just looked at him with a wry eye and nodded.

When Jack got to the Jukebox he put it on pause, then carefully rolled it away from the wall.

"See, I had it made with the optional caster wheels as well. This beauty is the cat's meow!"

Once he had it away from the wall, he pointed to an ornate brass metal plate fixed to the back. It was tufted at the upper ends and epaulets at the lower corners.

"Jack Humbolt - Jack's Beach Bar - 1935"

"I had that personalized brass plate made for me by Willie Sanchez down on the docks. He does a lot of work for the entire boating industry here in Key West, you know?" Jack explained.

Mark chimed in "That's so cool!". It wasn't a knee jerk polite response. It was an earnest statement. It was more than plain that he was sincere and excited about it. Rightfully so, as well. This was something else. The jukebox, or "coin-operated phonograph" was the coolest thing, and both Blackheart and Mark were entirely taken by it.

"You know, I'd love to have a juke…, er, coin operated phonograph, just like this one, in my house! Wouldn't that be off the charts, Blackheart?"

"Off the charts?" asked Jack with a polite smile. "You guys use some different terms! Where are you from, San Francisco or Seattle? Someplace far away from here, no doubt!"

Both Mark and Blackheart laughed along with Jack, and Mark placed his hand on Jack's shoulder. "Actually, we're both from New England, Connecticut to be exact. However, we met here in Key West, ironically. Blackheart is from Mystic, the old whaling seaport!"

"Mystic?" Jack replied. "That's an old seafaring town if there ever was one! A lot of captains from there came here and built their winter homes here, between fifty and one hundred years ago. Captains from the whole New England coast did. Mystic, New London, New Bedford, Providence, Newport, Chatham, Boston, Gloucester, Provincetown, Hyannis, Portsmouth, Portland, Bar Harbor, you name it. Just look at those houses on Margaret, Elizabeth, Francis, Southard, Fleming, and Division Street! Those big houses that look like they're from New England were designed by architects from up there, commissioned by the captains themselves! There's a lot of New England in this little rock just off the Tropic of Cancer, alright!"

Blackheart grinned "Yup! I'm from Mystic. I'm a captain as well! Runs in the veins. As a matter of fact, I sailed from here to Mystic a few years ago. Then on up to the Canadian border, less than a half mile from New Brunswick. Took us around eight months to do it, but I wouldn't trade it for the world! What a great time!"

Then he continued to marvel at the jukebox. "Jeeze! I can't get over this! It's stunning!"

"Yeah, like I say, it cost a pretty penny for that coin operated phonograph! Set me back almost two hundred and fifty bucks!" Jack volunteered. "But some things you can't put a price tag on, can you?"

He pushed it back to the wall and restarted it. It was playing Christmas songs, as it was the holiday season. It was funny to hear the records hiss and pop with their imperfections of early vinyl. It was also curious to hear Christmas songs from a different era. Many were the same, they had stood the test of time. Yet others apparently had fallen by the wayside over the years.

Hearing songs that were still played in his regular time, Mark wondered if he were listening to here was the original versions. Then again, he knew that a lot of the traditional holiday songs had been around for hundreds of years. Songbooks and families going door to door, singing to their unexpecting friends, keeping the traditional carols alive.

"Hark The Herald Angels Sing" had just come on with a nasally male voice singing in a piney fashion. It was all very melancholy, yet, at the same time, it was irritating to his twenty-first-century ear.

They went back to the bar and had a few more of the Royal beers. Jack seemed like a great guy and they all got on quite well. Over the next hour, several other patrons came in, mostly locals, and Jack knew them all.

A bit after midnight, Mark reminded Blackheart that he needed to get back for work in the morning, even if it was over eighty years in the future. Blackheart nodded. Mark paid the tab, and they headed back to his place.

Once inside, Mark extended his hand which Blackheart shook, saying, "I'm just flabbergasted. Seriously flabbergasted!" At which point everything started spinning again and, in a few seconds, they were back in Mark's regular time house.

"Blackheart, you can't tell anyone about this. You're the only friend I have that I could share this with."

"You have my word, my friend," Blackheart assured him. "Besides, everyone would think I'm taking up screenwriting!" They burst into laughter together over that remark.

Seriously however, Blackheart was a traditional New Englander when it came to this. His word was his bond. It was as solid as an anvil. Mark knew his newfound secret was secure with Blackheart.

Mark's day at the Sidecar Bar was uneventful, your basic average day. Or at least as average a day as could happen in Key West. Around one in the afternoon, in walks a man in a white bathrobe and slippers. The white bathrobe augmented his black skin tone. On the other hand, perhaps it was his pigmentation that highlighted the bathrobe? Either way, he lit up like the lighthouse's Fresnel lens. He was a walking, talking human beacon.

He strolled in as though he were a regular local, a degree short of owning the place. Mark's head jerked back slightly at first sight of the man. How couldn't it? The room literally lit up with his grand entrance.

"Good morning!!!" The man proclaimed in a booming baritone voice, and accent of upper class British public school education. He was clearly full of energy, thoroughly invigorated with the new day at hand. Mark was thinking that it's one in the afternoon and he's been up for hours. This fellow seemed to have awoken not all that long ago, at least judging by his attire.

Mark was his polar opposite. In a white shirt, bow tie and black slacks, he was ready for almost anything. He greeted the man professionally and politely.

"Good day, sir, and how can I assist you?"

In a mighty but respectful voice, the man replied, "Why, I'll have the same thing I was having last night!"

"I'm sorry, sir, I wasn't working last night," Mark said with a thin smile, head cocked to the side slightly.

The man stepped back and looked at Mark. "No, I don't suppose you were the man making me cocktails last evening, were you? Hmmm. Well then! It's warm out, so today seems like a gin and tonic might be in order, as a substitute for the morning tea they were out of, back where I'm staying, The Pier House. They had the gall to tell me that the continental breakfast had been over for nearly two hours," he said, disgruntledly.

Mark chuckled and replied, "Gin and tonic?"

"Indeed sir! However, make it with that Monkey 47 Gin, if you please!"

The Monkey 47 gin is made in the Black Forest in Germany, of all places, and not many people know about it. It's quite a potent gin at 47% alcohol and flavored with forty-seven botanicals, hence the name.

"Monkey 47, eh? You know your gin, sir," Mark stated to the man in the bathrobe as he mixed his elixir.

"Ha ha! Don't you know it? You can trust that fact as it was coin of the realm. Take that to the bank, sir!" He stated with a harrumph and a little chuckle.

It dawned on Mark that the man with the upper crust English accent reminded him of Sidney Greenstreet, the portly actor in many of Humphrey Bogart's films.

A cruise ship customer arrived, making the bar rounds in the three hours he was in port. He obviously had already made a stop or two and The Sidecar was at least his third. Mark knew the type well, harmless and just out for a fun time in Key West.

"I'll have a martini, please! Beefeaters, if you have it?" Then in a joking tone, he added, "Shaken not stirred! HA HA HA!"

"Sure," Mark replied. Things were shaping up to be a gin-soaked afternoon.

Mark entered each of their tabs under the names Bathrobe and Cruise Ship Drunk in the register. Mark came up with mental names for his customers. For him, it killed two birds with one stone. First, gave names to the customers that were appropriate. Second, they also had a kick of humor to them. After he applied Bathrobe and Cruise Ship Drunk as his cerebral and business brandings for these two, he actually did laugh out loud.

With his order placed, Cruise Ship Drunk started to relax and check out his surroundings. He then looked at Bathrobe. The realization of what he saw caught him way off guard. He hadn't noticed when he arrived on his martini quest. At that point he was focussed on Mark and placing his order.

"What the fuck? Dude! You're in a bathrobe!" Cruise Ship Drunk proclaimed.

"I am indeed, sir. Slippers as well, I might add," Bathrobe replied, lifting his highball glass with a polite cheer, a nod, a smile and a sip.

"You can't go around in a bathrobe. They'll pick you up!" Cruise Ship Drunk continued, shaking his inebriated head.

"Well, it's like this, my good man. I closed this fine establishment last evening at four in the morning. I suppose that would have been this morning, wouldn't it? Be that as it may, I was denied morning tea at The Pier House, where I'm staying. They said it was too late. In need of some sort of recovery, I retreated to the shower, which was quite invigorating, I'll assure you. Upon exiting the shower, I toweled off, then put on my robe and slippers and went down to the front desk. They, like yourself, seemed horrified. I told them it was nothing to be horrified about. I was in my bathrobe and slippers. The ladies at the pool outside had on far less. Regardless of that, they still seemed to be in a fluster about it, so I thought, as they couldn't supply me with tea, or even the American tradition of coffee, I'd just as soon head here for a bit of the hair of the dog, so to speak HAHA!" Once again, he raised his highball glass in a toast. "Cheers, old man!"

"The cops will stop you on the street and say, 'Who do you think you are walking the streets in a bathrobe?' Then they'll cart your ass away," Cruise Ship Drunk warned.

"I will tell them that I am Lord William T .Sanderson-Gardiner III and I hail from Wandsworth, a borough of London. I'll also tell them the same I did at the hotel, that I have seen many a young lady walking down the street with bikinis that are microscopic, to my delight I might add! My bathrobe is made with more material on it than forty of those bikinis, so there really shouldn't be an issue of any kind!"

"So what's your story?" Mark asked Bathrobe, as he slowly slid Cruise Ship Drunk's martini across the bar.

"My father had been the Earl of Wandsworth. He was kind of blackballed... pun intended, when he fell in love and married my mother, Alice Haddingley, a common black woman from Barbados. You are currently talking to the by-product of that notorious, and somewhat scandalous liaison, my good man!"

"You must be The Earl of Bathrobe!" Cruise Ship Drunk chimed in without mockery, but full of jest.

"Oh it's a fine piece of material, I assure you of that, sir. I bought it at Harrods."

Noticing that Cruise Ship Drunk looked a bit puzzled, Mark kicked in, "It's a very high-end store in London." Still a bit confused, Cruise Ship Drunk nodded nonetheless. He realized that Mark and Bathrobe traveled in different circles than he did.

Over the course of the afternoon, Cruise Ship Drunk paid his tab and was off to his ship, fearing if he waited any longer, he might be left behind and stranded in Key West. Things could be worse. He gave Mark his phone to take pictures of himself with Bathrobe before scampering out the door and down the street.

After several more Monkey 47 gin and tonics, Bathrobe, or Lord William T. Sanderson-Gardiner III, if you please, handed Mark a Barclay's Visa card with the name "Earl of Wandsworth" printed under his embossed name. His tab was $76.45 and he added gratuity to make it an even $100, which was more than fair. After signing the slip he spouted "And a good day to you sir! Oh… and a Happy Christmas to you! May Father Christmas treat you well!"

"And to you as well Lord Sanderson-Gardner! Also, thank you very much."

Lord Bathrobe stopped and acknowledged Mark with a slight nod of his head. He could tell that Lord Bathrobe honestly was surprised that a Yank would even know how to address nobility, much less do so. With a smile, he was gone. Mark went to the window with the sole purpose of watching the pedestrians reactions when they saw him. He walked as proudly and with the same confidence and distinction as the King did in the *Emperor's New Clothes*. The reactions of those on the street were the same as those in the story as well.

Mark watched until Lord William T. Sanderson-Gardiner was out of sight. He shook his head, chuckling to himself thinking "Just another day in Key West."

A couple of minutes later, Blackheart burst through the door.

"I came to see when you are getting off. There's something you need to see!"

"I'm off in five minutes. What's up?"

"Good! I'll just show you. It's something you just *have* to see!" Blackheart exclaimed. He was clearly quite excited. "Okay, great!" regaining his composure, then he continued "There's a mounted police man talking to a black guy in a bathrobe down the street!"

"That's the Earl of Wandsworth! Is he in trouble or something? He just left here," Mark stated.

"Earl of Wandsworth? Really? Trouble? No, they're both laughing! But it's one of those scenes best described as 'Only in Key West.' A mounted policeman talking to a guy in a bathrobe at almost six o'clock at night, both of them laughing."

"Yep, only In Key West!" nodded a smiling Mark. "So what's up?"

"You have to see this for yourself!"

Mark finished up and they headed up Duval Street. When they got to the antique store, Blackheart pointed and said, "In here!"

They entered the shop. Like many antique stores, inventory was immersed with merchandise everywhere. Apparently, their destination was near the back of the shop. Blackheart blazed the trail, clearly knowing his way around the maze of over-abundance. The scattered antiques made aisles into crooked alleyways, expensive and fragile obstacles jutting out from every direction.

When they finally got to the back of the store, there were four old jukeboxes.

"Oh! So you're on a jukebox kick after our little adventure last night! Cool stuff!" Mark exclaimed when he saw the four of them amongst the clutter.

Blackheart smiled, "Take a look at these a little more closely. They are all gorgeous. I'm actually thinking of buying one," he said.

"Really? They're not cheap, not by any stretch of the imagination," Mark chimed in looking at a price tag on one.

"No, they're not cheap, but retake a closer look. Those two on the end are older. One's a Rock-Ola, the other a Wurlitzer."

Mark took a closer look, then gasped in amazement.

"Holy shit! This Wurlitzer is the same model they had at Jack's, 78's and all! Looks just like it too! Probably, like the one in Jack's, over eighty years down the pike, a bit worn, naturally, but nice!" Mark commented on the old, kind of beat up jukebox.

"Check out the power chord in the back. Granted, it's a standard 110-volt plug and all, but there's something about it." Blackheart said, a curious tone to his voice. "Go ahead, it rolls easily with those optional caster wheels."

Mark grasped the jukebox on both sides. It rolled out easily, just as Blackheart said it would. Everything there was still tight quarters, but Mark was agile and wiggled his way so that he could clearly see the rear.

When he looked at the back of the box, he realized that checking the power cable was nothing but a ruse set up by Blackheart. There, in the middle of the box, was an old, tarnished, heavy brass plate. It was tufted on the upper corners with epaulets on the two lower corners. It wasn't easy to read with the tarnish built up over the decades, but it wasn't impossible either.

It read, "Jack Humbolt - Jack's Beach Bar - 1935."

Mark looked back at Blackheart in amazement, his jaw dropping wide open.

"Now you know why I want to buy it," Blackheart said with a warm smile. "It will never fit on my boat. How about if I buy it and we keep it at your house?"

Without hesitation, Mark replied, "Deal," and shook Blackheart's hand.

The floor manager waltzed up to them, batted his eyelashes, and said "Back to see that jukebox again, eh? Twice in one day. You must be really taken with it. It's fully functional, never been restored, and as I understand it, it spent fifty years at a local restaurant, then was in a private home until the owner passed away. We obtained it at an estate sale."

"Yeah, we do like this one. Let's see. You have it listed for four grand. I'll give you twenty-eight hundred right now in cash."

"Come on over to my office and let's see what we can do with that."

The friendly negotiation went on at the manager's desk. Blackheart didn't get the price he offered, and the manager didn't get the four grand he had it listed at either. However, they both had a deal that they were happy with and the coin-operated phonograph would be delivered in the next few days.

"The first thing I'm going to do is polish up that brass plate and make it look brand new again!" Blackheart said excitedly as they headed out the door.

"Let's head to the Cork and Stogie and cheer this purchase with a beer!" suggested Mark. They then turned left and headed towards the quiet section of Duval Street.

It was a few days since Mark had seen Glades. On the last voyage back with Blackheart, he didn't see her at all. This was a weird thing. Here he was having this affection for a woman who was living more than eighty years earlier. As surrealistic as that may have been, he wanted to see her again. It was a bright, sunny morning. and it was time to jump.

Jump. That was the term he chose for it. He concentrated, everything blurred, and off he went. He was back in his home in December 1935. He went outside, got on his bike, and headed over to see Glades.

Glades was late getting up that day and still in bed when Mark arrived. He knocked on her door and she arose quite groggy. Inviting Mark in, she started the percolator. A percolator! Mark had seen the last of these in use when he was young. His parents had one but had replaced it when he was nine or ten.

The coffee was good. Unlike the rest of the nation, here it wasn't just coffee, it was American coffee, in order to distinguish it from the various styles of Cuban coffees. Interestingly enough, they both took it black. Mark joked, "I'm very particular about my coffee, you know Glades? You must pour it at a forty-five-degree angle, or I'll throw it off the porch, to the street below!" They both laughed.

It was a gorgeous morning, and Glades was beaming. She made breakfast for the two of them, and they enjoyed it on her outside deck, one story above the corner store, overlooking Fish Bone Lane. The sun was shining and there was a cool December breeze traversing the deck, as they enjoyed the view, breakfast, and their coffee.

"It's a beautiful morning and such a wonderful view of this area of Old Town," Mark spoke in a sigh.

"Old Town? What's Old Town? I never heard the term before," Glades replied

Mark was taken aback for a moment. Why doesn't she know Old Town, he thought? Maybe it's not old enough yet? Heck, it's over eighty years younger than in his own time. He had to think quickly.

"Oh, I guess I call it Old Town because it looks old to me. Like a tropical old New England town, I guess. You know I'm from New England, after all. Key West has a very large New England architectural influence that I'm constantly reminded of every day. I love it! It's the best of both worlds."

Mark was able to diffuse the apparent gaff quite efficiently. The question remained in his mind as to when it started being called Old Town.

After breakfast, they went for a walk together down to the docks, which were only a block away. The last time they went to the Raw Bar, which was pretty similar to the way it was his own time. Today, they were further west, just bordering the dock and a trailer park at the end of William Street. The trailers were in good shape. Mark was amazed at their condition and immediately imagined what they would be selling for in his time. Some were art deco, in an Airstream style. As they walked by, he noticed that the stainless steel trailers carried the name Bowlus on them. He wondered if these would later become Airstreams. The family resemblance was uncanny. Others were made of wood. Mark imagined that they would fit perfectly in the movie "It's A Wonderful Life." He was thinking it would be great to walk through there to take pictures of them. However, he was with Glades, and explaining an iPhone to his 1935 girlfriend wasn't on his agenda for the time being.

They arrived at the dock where in his time was the bar Schooner Wharf. The building was there and the second story had an office. That office would burn off only several years before Mark arrived in Key West in his own time, but he had seen pictures of it. Here he was though, in 1935, and the building was a fish processing plant. Fishing boats were unloading their catches, and inside the open walls, men were cutting fish. It was a bustling environment, loud voices booming through the building. Mark was clearly impressed. Glades was distracted, taken in by the boats in the harbor. Mark was as quick as a gunslinger and rapidly pulled out his phone and took a few pictures. It was perfect timing. He got in eleven pictures.

They continued walking down the dock. The building that Mark knew to be Jimmy Buffett's studio was actually an ice house. It looked like an ice house in his regular lifetime, however, here it actually was. The one thing that struck him about it was that the doors were open and fishermen were actively walking in and out, picking up ice to keep their catch fresh. On extremely few occasions in his own time, Mark saw activity there. Once he saw Country singer George Strait leaving there. He later saw him at an art gallery on Duval, purchasing a painting by a Philippine artist named Milan. Of course, he had heard the notorious stories of Toby Keith spending a month recording there and eating lunch at Schooner Wharf every day. He, no doubt, got the inspiration for his song "I Love This Bar" from daily performer Michael McCloud playing a song he had written two decades prior, "Tourist Town Bar." Mark never saw Toby Keith. The studio was always shut tight as a drum, pun intended. In 1935 the ice house, however, was a nucleus of rapid activity. The contrast only made him smile.

They headed up Greene Street. On the right, the Coca Cola plant was also hopping with activity. He only knew it as an abandoned facility. Earlier that year, in his own time, they had razed the building in favor of expensive condominiums. Here, however, old-style trucks were pulling in and out, loaded with soda, returning to get replenished for more deliveries, blue exhaust smoke puffing from their entrails as they lumbered down the street.

Glades and Mark continued up Greene Street passing The Victoria Restaurant where they worked. It was coming up on one in the afternoon and the place was busy with the lunch rush. They both looked at it and laughed, shaking their heads. No point in even talking about it; their mutual look said it all. They just kept walking.

They crossed Duval and up to Sloppy Joe's Saloon. Heading inside, they waved hello to Skinner. Mark ordered a Royal and Glades ordered a Manhattan. Sitting at the bar, they chatted for a bit. Suddenly, a couple of boisterous men came briskly through the door, laughing and carrying on.

It was Josie Russell, Skinner hollered out "Hey Boss! What you having," Everyone in the bar knew him, and as Mark and Glades sat observing, Mark picked up immediately that he was the owner when Skinner addressed him as "Boss."

"A couple of cold beers please, Skinner!" he hollered in a friendly tone.

Skinner pulled out two Royals from below the counter, opened them, and laid them on the bar for Mr. Russell and his friend.

"Everything okay while I was gone?"

"Jus fine sah!" Skinner replied in his African-American Southern accent of the era. "We did have an incident, or two, but nothing ol' Jack couldn't get in line right quick." At which point he raised his baseball bat from behind the bar and laughed.

Josie Russell laughed as well. "Good to hear! We had a great time down in Havana these last couple of days!"

His friend then piped in with a booming "We have not had a good time in Havana ever!" He laughed hard, then took a big pull on his ice cold Royal.

Mr. Russell's friend was in his mid-thirties, a big frame but by no means overweight, and sported with a mustache. Mark started to wonder as soon as he saw him. Could it be...??? He pretty much knew it was, only here he was, in the flesh, walking, talking, moving about and swigging a beer.

Suddenly, the friend of Mr. Russell looked at Mark directly from across the bar. This was direct eye-to eye contact, his stare serious, unwavering, and aimed directly at Mark.

"I know you from somewhere! Where is it?" he blurted out. There was nothing subtle about it, bordering on a command rather than a polite inquiry. It wasn't aggressive, per say, but no doubt quite assertive. He then swaggered around the bar with determination. He was a man on a specific quest. Not angry, just determined.

"You know him? Word around town is that he's some kind of famous author," Glades added, as he came around the bar at a good clip.

"So where do I know you from? I know your face. Was it Paris? Havana? It wasn't here in Key West, I know that. My name is Ernest. It wasn't in the war. That was too long ago. However, it wasn't recent either."

Mark, of course, had never met Ernest Hemingway. His mind was racing. So far, in his time traveling adventures, which only amounted to a few weeks, he had been traveling back to 1935 Key West. What if, in his future, he traveled to another time and place that preceded Key West in 1935?

"How do you do, sir? My name is Mark Straight." Mark extended his right hand and Ernest grabbed and shook it firmly, looking him directly in the eye. It was a firm, sure handshake, conveying the same assertiveness that his cannon report-like voice booming across the bar, did fifteen seconds earlier did. Mark continued.

"I'm not sure off hand. However, I will say this, Mr. Hemingway, I did meet your wife recently. She was out on your lawn with your sons and governess. Actually, she thought she was coming to my aid, thinking I was having trouble. I wasn't, fortunately. We had a nice, short conversation. As it turned out, I mixed the drinks you were drinking several days prior at The Victoria Restaurant. This is Glades, she was your server."

"Server?" Glades asked.

102

"Oh, I don't know where that came from! Waitress!" Another twenty-first-century piece of vernacular, slipping into a twentieth-century conversation. One of these days it will get him, he thought. Not this time. The determined writer was fixed on knowing from where he knew Mark from.

Ernest mentally noted that Mark addressed him formally by his surname when he himself never used it in his introduction. Chances were good that this Straight fellow, unlike the majority of this town, was educated and could conceivably be well read. Mark Straight knew who he was, which in Hemingway's mind, was a point in his favor. It also may have reinforced the hunch that they very well may have met previously. He certainly did seem familiar but from where?

"Just call me Ernest," he said, waving off the Mr. Hemingway, but Mark could tell that he was flattered by his recognition. The fact was, three-quarters of this fishing village didn't know how to read, much less know who the man was. Most knew him as a referee at the boxing matches at that bordello on Thomas and Petronia streets, just a short walk from his house.

"Pauline! Yes, she's a very compassionate woman. However, The Vic' is not where I know you from. Not too recent, not too far back, and not from Key West."

"Well, I grew up in Connecticut and spent some time in Brooklyn."

"Brooklyn? Why you must know the Wheeler Shipyard then?"

"Wheeler Shipyard? Sure, I've heard of it."

"Yes, it's by the Brooklyn Navy Yard!"

"Exactly!"

The Brooklyn Navy Yard had been sold off to private enterprise long ago. In his time, the Brooklyn Navy Yard had been developed into expensive condominiums, echoing names from the former shipyard. Long gone were the shipyards that built ships for the Navy. Alas, long gone also was the Wheeler shipyard. However, this was 1935, and what Mark knew from the future didn't pertain to this era.

"They built my boat, Pilar, there. She's a fine craft. It has a special engine used only for trawling. That's a forty horsepower Lycoming, plus a seventy-five horsepower Chrysler for regular use. We just had it down Havana way for a week. Last spring, we took her over to Bimini in the Bahamas."

He took a long pull on his Royal, then continued.

"Paris? Was it in Paris maybe?" he said rubbing his chin. Then, pointing his finger up in the air, he asked directly and somewhat intensely, "Gertrude Stein! Do you know Gertrude Stein?"

Mark gave a quick knee jerk answer, without too much thought it came out.

"Of course I know Gertrude Stein!"

What Mark meant, was that he knew of Gertrude Stein's works, as well as a bit about the novelist, playwright, and poet herself. However, Ernest interpreted his answer as meaning he knew her personally.

"It must have been at a get together at her apartment in Paris then! There's an interesting crowd if there ever was one, wouldn't you say? Scott Fitzgerald, Pablo Picasso, Henri Matisse, James Joyce, Sinclair Lewis, John Dos Passos, the list just went on and on! It was the literature and art Mecca of Paris. A curious crowd indeed, isn't it? Some called us 'The Lost Generation.'"

Mark wasn't sure which way to go. Should he just ride along with the misunderstanding and play his cards, hoping Hemingway wouldn't catch on? Or maybe he should just come clean and let Hemingway know that he only knew of Gertrude Stein?

He quickly decided to roll with it, then change the subject before Hemingway went too much further in depth with details.

"She has a great salon there, doesn't she?" Mark stated. He realized quickly that he made a statement that really left himself wide open. He had no clue what her salon looked like, only that it must have been a very cool gathering place.

"Is it ever! 27 Rue de Fleures! What a place!" he said with a broad smile. "You know? About a year before I came to Key West, I had two steamer trunks stored at the Hotel Ritz. They're filled with all kinds of things. I'm hoping I have two notebooks on people and places regarding the goings on in Paris. I think that's where I left them. One of these days, I'll put together a memoir."

Mark was thinking, Holy shit! 'Sometime' would turn out to be in the fifties! Hemingway did recover the notes and started working on "A Movable Feast," which was posthumously released a few years after his death.

Mark now looked at Glades, then back at Hemingway. This time it was he who took a large pull on his Royal, saying, "Paris is certainly a beautiful city! Where did you live there, Ernest?" He was playing with matches and gasoline, and he knew it. On the other hand, he had spent a fair amount of time in Paris himself, visiting several times, and knew it somewhat well.

"I lived on the third floor above the Bal au Printemps, a dance club at 74 Rue du Cardinal Lemoine. It's in the Latin quarter if you're familiar with that. Joyce lived across the street from me. Later I had an apartment in Montparnasse. "

"Joyce? Not sure I can place her," Mark interceded. He was really striking the matches too close to the proverbial open can of gasoline. He knew exactly who Hemingway was talking about, but was hoping to derail the conversation in order to save his own skin.

"No! No! Not 'she', damn it! James Joyce, the Irish writer!" Hemingway burst out, a touch angry. A second after he said it, he burst out laughing. "Ha! Ha! Joyce! Of course. I empathize with you, old man!" slapping him on the back and taking another pull on his Royal. "Hey, Skinner! Can I buy these two folks a beer, please? I'll have one myself as well."

Old man. Mark chuckled at the name. Here he was, thirty-nine years old and with Hemingway, hoping to bullshit his way far enough to be enjoyed, but not far enough to be caught. If Hemingway discovered he was playing him, he very well may deck him right then and there. He had a well-established reputation, founded on fact. Hopefully, Mark's five-year elder status might cut him some slack, should push come to shove.

No, it wouldn't. Not with Hemingway. Perhaps if F. Scott Fitzgerald had been the one whom Mark was talking with. But Hemingway was just too brash to take any wool being pulled over his eyes. He'd deck him, no doubt about it. Especially with a few beers in him, and who knows what he had drunk before walking into the joint? By the sound of things, they had just cruised in from Havana. The long trip, no doubt, would have been fortified with alcohol.

Skinner brought the beers over and cracked them open. Ernest raised his beer to Mark and Glades, his new found friends.

"To Paris!" The entire bar raised their drinks and toasted with Ernest.

"TO PARIS!!!!" the entire bar hollered out.

Ernest then turned to Mark and asked, "So tell me, Mark, how do you know Gertrude?"

He was in over his head at this point. No question about it. He raised his can up to his lips and took a large pull on it. With a smile, he said, "Ernest, hold that thought, I have to hit the head. I'll explain when I get back!" He used the nautical term for the bathroom, hoping to hit a good nerve with Ernest, the great yachtsman, known for his prowess with his craft the Pilar. Time to take leave and regroup. If he faltered now, which was highly likely, he knew he'd be lying on the floor, looking at the ceiling, with his teeth would be scattered around him like a pack of spilled Chicklets.

"Ha Ha! It's always good to reminisce about Paris! I'll look forward to hearing your angle." Ernest replied jovially.

Mark was in Ernest's good interests still, but what next? It's sink or swim time, and Mark didn't have the information that Ernest was looking for. How was he going to get out of this gracefully and without crashing and burning with his favorite author of all time? What possessed him to get into the mental sparring match with his own head on the chopping block?

As he entered the men's room, he wasn't sure how he got himself up on this high wire without a net. What the hell was he thinking? Sparring with one of America's finest literary figures, on a subject that was Hemingway's theoretical thesis. Here, Mark only had a brief smattering degree of knowledge on the subject. It's a wonder he actually had gotten as far as he had. How would he get out of this? If Hemingway discovered the reality of the fact that Mark had not been to Gertrude Stein's, or ever met any of the people who did, Hemingway would see him as a complete phony, and view him with disdain and disgust for eternity.

What could he do to clear himself of the spider web he just weaved?

When Mark entered the men's room, there was some drunk guy in there but that didn't matter. It was time to jump. That was the only way to resolve the potential mess he could be in. This was going to be a different kind of jump. The only jumps he's done thus far was back and forth between his time and 1935 Key West. Here he was looking at jumping across the Atlantic Ocean to Paris in the 1920's from 1935. A jump within a jump would be an adventure if there ever was one, but it had to be done. The consequences of Ernest Hemingway figuring out he was a fraud could result in him losing those teeth. Mark didn't relish that idea, and the idea of visiting a 1935 dentist with teeth in his hand, in hope that they could be put back in place, terrified him more.

"Okay, so let's go with April in Paris, 1922," he thought. "April 21st. A Friday, say 10 am."

Mark closed his eyes and off he went. The drunk's jaw dropped as Mark suddenly vanished before his very eyes! Puff! He was gone.

He materialized in a men's room in some Parisian cafe, or bar. Men's room to men's room. What a way to do his first jump within a jump! He didn't recognize it at first. He was alone. When he landed he was looking directly at the sink. The fixtures were clearly non-American, quite ornate and reading "Froid" and "Chaud" on the faucet handles. Looking around he saw framed advertising posters in French, on the wall. One had the name Gitanes, at a fifteen-degree angle, with the letters sloping from large to small, on a light blue background. Below the lettering was a black silhouette of a woman in a full-length dress, arching back, with a tambourine in mid performance. A gypsy woman, no doubt, he thought. Yes, he was in Paris, alright.

Suddenly a man came out of one of the stalls with a small bag.

He spoke to Mark in French, which apparently he already knew Mark could get by with.

"Good afternoon Mr. Straight. Welcome to Paris. My name is Francois Arnaux and I am your assistant. I have this satchel for you which has both clothes and money. Additionally, you'll see the address where you'll be staying, 35 Rue de la Gare. It is an apartment we always have at the ready for the travelers such as yourself. Right now you are in the cafe Les Deux Magots. It is a cafe frequented by literary circles. Any questions?"

Mark was surprised and fortunately did speak a bit of French, which he took back when he was in school, years earlier. On a recent stay of six months in Paris, albeit over eighty years in the future, he brushed up and was able to get by without too much problem.

"Merci, Monsieur Arnaux. Enchanté! Merci beaucoup de votre aide et de votre générosité."

(Thank you Mr. Arnaux. A pleasure to meet you! Thank you very much for your assistance and generosity.)

François continued, "I forgot! You are in apartment number seven on the third floor. My apartment is across the hall, number five. Also, from here on, just call me Francois."

Mark shook his hand and reconfirming. "Ainsi, vingt-deux rue de la gare, troisième étage, numéro sept."

François smiled and nodded in agreement. "Exactement, Monsieur Straight. If you need anything, I'm at your service, across the hall at the apartment."

Mark was still puzzled. "You're my assistant? How did you know to meet me here?"

François laughed. "A good friend of both of ours told me!"

"Merci encore François... Oh, before you leave!"

"Oui monsieur?"

Mark reached into the satchel for the bill fold. He was amazed to see it was stuffed with an assortment of bills, as well as a side pouch which contained coins. Without thought, or hesitation, he handed François thirty Francs.

"Merci Beaucoup, Monsieur!" It was more than obvious that Monsieur Arnaux very much appreciated the gratuity. Thirty francs went a very long way in 1922 Paris!

In English and with a wry smile, Mark asked him, "Oh, one question for you Francois. Where the hell am I?"

François laughed and answered in English. "Ha Ha! Exactly where you wanted to be Monsieur Straight! That's why I am here to assist you! I know all of this is new to you. As I mentioned earlier, you're in the Cafe Deux Magots, in the men's toilet. A funny, yet actually the perfect place for you to land for us to rendezvous!"

They shook hands and François walked out of the cafe. He thought, The Cafe Deux Magots? Holy crap!

How bizarre is this? Mark was thinking. He jumps to a Paris cafe in 1922 and he has a minion waiting to assist him. This time traveling had it's serious advantages, but it also was hazed in mystery. How did this all come about after all?

Heading through the cafe's interior, Mark was quite taken by it all. Ornate, classic, and beautiful, as one would expect a Parisian cafe to be. It was brightly lit by the sunlight alone and the walls were white, which highlighted the sunlight. There were a few pillars stretching to the ceiling, which had to be fifteen feet high. Pastries were in glass cases. The cafe was bustling and permeated with joyful talk and laughter. He pulled out his Roskopf pocket watch and saw it was 10:13 am. A good time for a crème. Outside seemed less crowded, so he continued through the restaurant to the sidewalk tables, all the while taking everything in, yet under the fog of meeting an assistant who hands him, among other things, a bag full of money. He found an empty table, where he sat with a good view of both the restaurant and the sidewalk.

The waiter arrived at the table with a bounce in his step and a cheerful disposition.

"Bonjour Monsieur! Comment pouvons-nous vous aider ce matin?"

"Oui! Bonjour! Puis-je avoir une crème et un croissant?" Mark replied.

He asked for the Parisian version of a latte, or a cafe con leche, and a croissant. The waiter smiled, nodded, and scurried off.

It was a beautiful morning, about seventy-five degrees, or twenty-four in Celsius, the local system, and sunny. Paris was bustling with vendors pushing carts up the street, and horse-drawn carriages carrying their passengers to their destinations. An accordion player was setting up to perform music in the far corner of the cafe.

The waiter returned briskly with the crème and the croissant.

"Here you are, sir! Your crème and croissant!" he said.

"Oh! You speak English?"

"Yes, Monsieur! We get a large amount of English speaking clientele here, from England, Ireland, and America, like yourself. You are from America, aren't you?"

"Indeed! Key West, by way of Brooklyn, New York, by way of Connecticut."

"Key West? Isn't that the tropical island railroad town with the long bridge going to it?"

"That's the one!" Mark laughed.

"It must be magnifique! A tropical island! Excusez-moi! My name is Marcel."

"I'm Mark, how do you do?"

They shook hands. Marcel was a pleasant guy with an easy smile and laugh. He looked up and said suddenly. "Oh look! Here's another American! Gertrude! Comment allez-vous?"

"Je vais bien, merci. Et toi?" Gertrude replied saying she was fine, and politely inquiring on how Marcel was.

"Oh! You must meet my new American friend, Mark!" Marcel excitedly stated.

"How do you do, Mark? I'm Gertrude."

Mark recognized her from pictures he had seen in his own time. "No! Not Gertrude Stein?" Mark stated as he rose from his chair.

"I'm afraid I'm guilty, so long as you're not the police or tax collectors!"

"Hardly, I'm a bartender," he stated smiling, shaking her hand. "I'd be honored for you to join me, if you're free and care to. I promise I'll be on my best behavior."

"Why not? Are you new here, perhaps? If so, you can fill me in on what's happening stateside, and maybe I can give you some insight on what it's like being an expat living in gay Paris." While she never cracked a smile, Mark picked up that this was her sense of humor. He knew from reading about her that she was stoic, as well as very direct and to the point.

Without hesitation, she pulled the chair out, sat down, and ordered a Perrier from Marcel.

No sooner than she was seated, the accordion player started playing a song Mark didn't recognize, although it was textbook Parisian music. That was unmistakable. The reality and surrealism started to set in. Here he was, sitting with Gertrude Stein, at a sidewalk cafe in Paris on an early morning in April 1922! Meanwhile, Ernest Hemingway is waiting on his return from the men's room at Sloppy Joe's in Key West, thirteen years in the future, to talk about a meeting which thus far, had yet to transpire. If that wasn't surreal, what was?

On an entirely different subject, Mark felt like he was adapting to this time traveling thing fairly well. He felt he did well with Ernest, up to the point he left. His plan was to stay in Paris a few days and gather some background information. After that, he'll then jump back into the bathroom at Sloppy Joe's to the moment he left, surprise the drunk in there, and have more information from Paris to continue the conversation with Ernest. He chuckled to himself. Here he was on a first name basis with Ernest Hemingway, of all people, and now on the cusp of being the same with Gertrude Stein. On the other hand, he was in Paris, 1922. The reality was that he never met Hemingway at this point, at least not in 1922. That would happen thirteen years in the future. The thought of this was mind boggling, but he knew he had to keep his wits about himself.

Marcel returned with the Perrier.

"A rose is a rose is a rose, Miss Stein," Mark said, raising his crème to her, quoting her famous poem.

She smiled and raised her glass. "To art and literature." She didn't show it, but inside she was flattered that this gentleman she had only been introduced to a few minutes earlier, was acquainted with her work.

"Art and literature! I concur wholeheartedly!"

They touched glasses in a toast.

"You know? Toasting with a Perrier is just fine, however cheering with a crème just doesn't seem right," Mark mentioned after they cheered.

Marcel was passing a few tables away, and Mark raised his finger. His eyebrows raised, and he smiled when Marcel caught sight and hustled over.

"Oui Monsieur Mark? How may I assist?"

"It's afternoon, a beautiful day, I'm at a sidewalk cafe in Paris, with exceptional company. I think it's time for a beer!"

"Oui, oui Monsieur! I have Biere de Paris, Kronenbourg, or La Belle Strasbourgeoise? I also have Beck's, Bittburger, and Hofbrau from Allemagne."

"I'll stick with a French beer today, Marcel. You have the same saying we do: 'when In Rome' in French, as we do in English! So here I am in Paris! I'll have a La Belle, please."

"La Belle! Très bon! Madame? Anything to go with your Perrier, Gertrude?"

"I'm good for the moment. Merci, Marcel."

116

Mark couldn't help but recall history, knowing that the Germans would be marching into Paris in eighteen years. In addition, he knew that this particular cafe would be frequented by German officers. No matter how much he loved German beer, he could not drink any here with the impending events, so many years still to come. It would be a cultural sacrilege to do so, especially sitting here with an American-Jewish woman. It didn't hurt that La Belle Strasbourgeoise was, indeed, a great beer on its own.

Mark and Gertrude sat and chatted about various writers and artists in Paris. He also filled her in on the life of a bartender. The beauty was that the decades really never changed the profession as far as day to day life goes. Granted, in Mark's regular time Key West had the potential to lean to the bizarre, such as Lord Sanderson-Gardner, walking into the Side Car in a bathrobe. However, meeting and entertaining people, being the consoling friend of someone in love or economic stress? Those unwritten rules transcended time.

Gertrude expressed interest in Key West. She thought that she'd love to ride on the Overseas Railway and asked Mark what it was like. The only way Mark had ever gotten to Key West was to drive the Overseas Highway, also known as Route 1, or flew in. That was in his regular time in the Twenty-First Century. Neither of these was an option in 1922. Accessing Key West was only available by either ship or train.

Mark could relate quite easily from his driving experiences, however, and took this liberty to describe the journey to his new friend Gertrude what it was like.

"The train to Key West is nothing short of amazing. Here you are, traveling over the ocean on a train. It is quite akin to what has been developing here in Paris really. Surrealism, you know? Rooted in Guillaume Apollinaire's cubism works! You'll see more and more of that here in time, I assure you.

"Anyway, this railroad, traversing the ocean mile by mile, island hopping over forty islands and over one hundred miles! You have the Atlantic Ocean on your left, and the Gulf of Mexico on your right. The water is simply amazing! You look out and see so many different colors, from dark blue, to aqua blue, to sand beige, to aqua green, to just plain green! It changes one day to the next. Tomorrow may well be another show entirely!

"The island towns you travel by are all different, yet similar. All of them have mangroves and all have variations of palm trees. Most of the keys have citrus plants we call key limes, highly acidic and quite small citrus fruits. Locals use as a condiment. The train makes a few stops. I guess it's a five-hour ride, or so from start to finish."

Mark really didn't know how long the ride itself took, but, with the times being 1922, he hoped his guesstimate seemed credible.

Gertrude interjected "That seems just fascinating Mark. Hopefully one day I'll make that trip on the train. It would be a great adventure to embark on! I very much appreciate you sharing a small portion of your life with me. It's something I've never come in contact with before."

She thought for a moment, then continued, "You know, you might enjoy coming to my salon Saturday night. I'd like to have you over. I have some interesting friends who stop by from time to time that I know you'll enjoy. They are artists and literary people, poets and authors alike. So, what do you say? Saturday evening around seven?"

Mark smiled and nodded. "Gertrude, I'd be honored. Thank you so much. It's so kind of you."

"Good," Gertrude stated in her matter of fact style. She pulled out a pencil and paper from her purse, jotting down her address for Mark: 27 Rue de Floures. "I have to run. It's been a pleasure meeting and exchanging ideas and experiences with you."

She got up, as did Mark. They cordially shook hands and his new acquaintance, Gertrude Stein, left the table, making a point to go up to Marcel to say good afternoon and express her gratitude.

"Wow. Class act," Mark thought.

There was a newspaper left on the table next to his. He glanced at the header, "Le Petit Parisien." He looked closer, then under the title, Vendredi, 21 Avril 1922.

It worked! It was a perfect time travel!

He had two days to himself in Paris! Then, tomorrow night at seven, an evening at Miss Stein's gathering of this week's cluster of The Lost Generation! He, of course, knew it from history, and now he was going to a gathering in a couple of days!

Here he was, Paris, April 1922. He just had a conversation with Gertrude Stein! How could this be happening? Again, why him? That question remained a vastly unopened query, but he refused to become absorbed in it. That was an instinct. It was an unknown source of knowledge, ingrained into his brain. After all, there was no field guide to time traveling! At least his mentor, Arthur, never fessed up to there being one. He felt that going forward, without more time pondering the "if's, how's, and why's" than necessary, was by far the more important, perhaps vital thing to do. He was bestowed this attribute somehow by fate. It wasn't really up to him to analyze it down to the smallest quark. Although he felt he may be here because of the need to answer Hemingway, fourteen years in the future, he also was beginning to feel there was more to it than that. Something put him here for a reason. It was his responsibility to go forth and see it through.

He waved to Marcel, then when he had his attention, Mark pointed to his La Belle Strasbourgeoise and Marcel gave a thumbs up.

A couple of days in Paris, 1922, was a splendid idea indeed.

There is a song "April in Paris," made many, many years ahead of the moment he was enjoying right now at Les Deux Magots. Mark knew it from Count Basie, recorded long before his actual time, having been released in 1957. It was a monumental album when it was released, and it had gone down in the annals of Jazz history as one of the all time classics.

The gentleman playing the accordion in the back had taken a break and Basie's "April In Paris" was flowing through his head. Here he was, April 21st 1922, in Paris. He still didn't understand the Time Traveling. However, though he was not clear on how, or why, he was becoming an adept with it. Instead of being in various stages of confusion and bewilderment, he was now quite, if not fully, somewhat at ease with it. He even was enjoying it. Here he was, on what he was calling to himself a "double jump": he went from his own time in the twenty-first century Key West, back to 1935, Key West, then to 1922, Paris, France. Definitely progress.

The overall plan in the Paris escapade was to gather knowledge, then head back to the moment where he disappeared in front of the drunk in the men's room in Sloppy Joe's, head back to the conversation at the bar with his new drinking buddy, Ernest Hemingway. Thinking of him as his drinking buddy was, of course, a far stretch, but he found it quite humorous and it made him laugh to himself.

He pulled out the Roskopf from his pants and flipped it open. 12:33. The trees along Saint Germain-des-Pres were all well into sprouting their Spring leaves, and a light breeze swept through in a casual, lazy way.

Mark got his bill, paid Marcel, and started off to his Parisian residence at 35 Rue de la Gare. It was a good walk, very invigorating, and it took over a half hour. It wasn't close, yet it wasn't too far either.

When he saw the address, he pulled the key Francois had given him earlier in the toilet at Les Deux Magots. The door was carved wood and painted blue, with its knob in the center of the door. He put the key in, twisted it, and the lock released.

"Troisième étage." Third floor, he recalled Francois saying. Number 7. It reminded him on the key. The stairs were narrow and winding. When he got to the third floor, there were three apartments in the hallway: 5, 6, and 7. As a sort of security, he looked at number 5 across the hall, recalling that was where Francois resided.

The apartment was adequate though not luxurious, yet it did have a homey feeling about it. It was more akin to an efficiency actually, though larger. Mark's first impression was that it was comfortable. It was one large room, located on the corner, with bay style windows on either side, offering shade optionally by sliding white lace curtains. The kitchen, set to the right when entering the apartment, had a wood burning stove, which could double as a heater. The bed was off to the left. It had curtains all the way around it; at this moment they were tied to the four posts that stretched up, pointing to the ceiling, about seven feet high. It was a large bed, very comfortable for overnight company. A heavy curtain separated it from the living room. Between the front door and the bed was an armoire. Mark opened it. Inside, there appeared to be brand new clothes. He pulled out a suit type jacket made of a coarse corduroy and tried it on. It was a tailored fit. He looked at the shoes. They looked to be about his size. He sat in one of the two living room chairs, which were on either side of a wood burning heater, between the windows. Next to it was a small bushel of wood. With both the stove and the heater, winter weather could be kept at bay. However, it was Springtime in Paris, and one was only needed to be utilized for those cooler April nights.

He took off his shoes and tried on a pair from the armoire. They were brand new and fit him perfectly, just as the jacket had.

Mark walked around the apartment looking down at his shoes. They were comfortable. Back at the armoire, he opened the drawers and found changes of clothing. The sizes were in metric, but all appeared to be his size.

This was one of the mysteries which was not understood by him at all. Baffling, actually. How did they know he was coming? How did they amass such a large amount of money for him? How did they know his sizes and measurements? How did François know to meet him in the toilet at Les Deux Magots? Who is this François, anyway? Certainly, a friend. How do you not consider someone a friend if they suddenly and unexpectedly appear to your aid with a satchel loaded with cash and a place to live? How did this apartment come about, anyway? Money, an apartment, tailor fit clothes, this was perplexing indeed, however perplexing in a very good way. All sorts of mysteries were gaining popularity in his mind.

Returning to the living room, he sat down and took off the shoes. A large grandfather clock was lazily ticking away. It read 1:23. Mark thought it was a good time to give the bed a test ride; perhaps a nap of a half hour or so would fit the bill.

The bed not too hard. The covers were ample and fluffy. He realized the apartment had a fragrance of lavender to it. Smiling, he closed his eyes and dozed off.

A knock at the door woke Mark up. He pulled out his Roskopf, opening it to see the time. 2:21. He had slept a little longer than intended.

"Un moment s'il vous plait," (One moment please) Mark called out. He rose from bed quickly and made his way to the door, attempting to straighten his hair, unkempt after his rest. He opened the door and at eye level was François and there was a taller man behind him. Looking down the stairway.

"Hey, François! How are you? What's up?" Mark said as he continued raking his disheveled hair with his hand.

"Très bien, merci! I have a friend of yours here."

The man turned around from looking down the stairway. It was Arthur!

"ARTHUR!!!" Mark exclaimed, extending his hand to Arthur, then Francois.

"You're getting the hang of all this, aren't you? 1935 Key West, now 1922 Paris. You're doing quite well, I must say! May we come in?" Arthur replied with a warm grin.

"Of course, of course! Entrez!"

They both entered. Separating the kitchen from the living room was a small bar, accommodating four. Both François and Arthur came in with a distinctive degree of familiarity. Without any hesitation, they sat at the bar. At the end of the bar, there were three bottles of wine, a large bottle of Perrier, plus a bottle of Pernod absinthe.

"Do yourself a favor and steer clear of the absinthe. It will take you places you've never been before, and most likely never want to revisit afterward. The hangover could last several days. Trust me, I know from experience." Arthur proclaimed with a laugh associated with someone who had a memorable, but unpleasant experience. The kind that had lessons to match.

He continued, "So you've been time traveling for a bit now, and you seem to be getting the hang of it."

"True. However, there remains a lot of mystery with it all. A lot of unanswered questions. Questions here, there, and everywhere. I have a feeling you know what I'm talking about."

"Rest assured, Mark. François, as your personal assistant, can be trusted 100%. He will never lie to you and his suggestions will only be for the wellbeing of yourself and The Organization of Time Travelers. And I assure you, your safety will always be paramount.

"'The Organization of Time Travelers'? Really?" Mark asked in a half joking, half mocking tone, and a slight laugh followed.

Arthur smiled. "I know it sounds hilarious. Frankly, it is a funny name. Some just call it the O.T.T. However, it is a registered company. It's a good organization, and we do our best to have everyone taken care of adequately. How do you think this apartment is paid for? Have you seen the clothes in the armoire? They didn't just appear. In the satchel that Francois gave you there was close to $1000. Do you have any idea how much that equates to in your time's money? At least $15,000. You know what that buys here in Paris, April 1922? A beer here in Paris today costs about a nickel if that. In other words, the cost of living here in this time is a pittance of what it is in your time. This flat is yours. It's in the company name, but it is yours. The company owns the building. You can come back in two, three ten years, and it's still your flat, no one else's. It will be maintained on a weekly basis when you are not here by François. We take good care of our own."

"This is amazing! That's one of the things I don't understand at all about this. Where does the money come from and why me?" Mark was truly astounded as he asked the perplexing query.

"Mark, there are mysteries none of us will ever understand. Religions believe in God. They all may have different names and beliefs, but they all believe in an entity they cannot see or speak with directly. Faith.

"As for us, we're not a religious society, however like religion, we too have a faith, so to speak. For starters, you can be of any faith, and be a time traveler. What we have found is that all time travelers have turned out to be exceptionally good people. There's no hate, greed, or bad traits among us. Oh, plenty have character, all right! We're no saints, believe me. A night out on the town, romance on the flight, sure! However, there are no devious or nefarious individuals among us. We harbor no criminals, those with bad intent. We have no idea why this is, but we're thankful and grateful. As in religion, we have faith it will continue.

126

"All time travelers are team players and the philosophy is the old adage 'One for all and all for one'. It's our creed. In the case of you and myself, I am your sponsor. I am here to answer questions. Bear in mind, not all questions will be answered at once, but in due time, providing we know the answer, of course."

"Can you tell me how you exist financially? Where does the money come from? It's an exorbitant amount. You say you have a company. What is it, in textiles? Stocks? Automotive? You understand my confusion, I'm sure. You're my sponsor?" Mark questioned.

"Well, to start off, Mark, be rest assured that all of our financial dealings are honest. Yes. I am your sponsor. I'll get to that in a bit.

"As I said, we're all good people. How people with such similar traits in ethics are gathered together and become time travelers, we don't know. The way we get our money is very simple and honest. Actually, it's the type of thing that will surely make you laugh. What we do is take advantage of our situation in life, which is that we are time travelers. It's a funny process that literally goes back and forth. One thing I didn't mention. All modesty aside, speaking matter of fact; all time travelers happen to possess the uncanny attribute of being very intelligent, coupled with a very high degree of common sense. It may sound unusual, but it's a wonderfully uncommon trait.

"Let's take today as an example. I'm in Paris, 1922. I have one thousand French Francs in my wallet. Very few of these Francs are made in 1922, most are from say 1900 – 1914 when World War I started. I'll have maybe 15% of these Francs that pre-date 1900 as well.

"Of course in your time, one thousand French Francs don't exist. In your time it's the Euro. In 1922 a French Franc was worth around twelve cents. Bear in mind that one French Franc could actually buy a few beers and a sandwich at a cafe in Paris.

"So, let's take that one French Franc, worth about twelve cents today, in 1922." Arthur reached into his pocket and pulled out a wad of French bills and pulled out a five French Franc note.

"Let's take this Five Franc note, worth close to one U.S. Dollar, in Paris right now. So, as a time traveler, what do I do, Mark?"

"I think you're getting at something. I'm not exactly sure what it might be though," replied Mark.

"Well, let's look at this particular bill itself. It's a Five Franc note. It was printed in 1909."

He paused and leaned forward, looking Mark dead in the eye before continuing slowly.

"Mark, do you have any idea what this note, which was obtained honestly, I assure you, is worth in your time?"

"I think I'm seeing where you are coming from, Arthur," Mark stated, smiling.

"So, a French Franc that we can buy here for pennies, we take back and sell in, say, your time period, for a substantial profit."

Arthur reached again into his pocket and pulled out a gold coin.

"This is a gold ten Franc coin. It cost us about two dollars. Keep in mind, that's two 1922 dollars. I take it back with me to the Twenty-First Century and you know what I can get for it?"

"You have me on the edge of my seat," Mark replied, laughing.

"We can get something like $330 to $350 for this coin. Our investment in it is pennies. Yes, this is the high side. So, say you have a standard coin of the realm. Let's see. Look, here's a 1913 ten Centime World Coin. We can get this for around one or two cents. When we bring it back, we can get around twelve or thirteen dollars for it on E-Bay."

"That's incredible! Isn't there a store we can sell them through?"

"No. We don't need to appear as anything other than individual collectors in the eyes of the government. We do similar things with postage stamps as well. The return is not as good, but who's going to be critical about a six hundred to one-thousand percent profit?"

Arthur was amazing in Mark's eyes, but he did have further questions.

"This is truly incredible Arthur. Understanding how it works going here to the Twenty-First Century is one thing, but how do you get that back to, say, here in 1922? It's not as though I could flash a C-note issued in 2017 at them in 1922," Mark inquired.

"Absolutely true! That's the second stage. Let's just take a look in my satchel." He pulled out his Louis Vuitton bag. It was a beautiful, gentleman's brown canvas bag with small Fleur de Lis emblems and LV initials in beige throughout, which had a fine stitched sturdy leather handle. Mark could tell by the way Arthur lifted it, that it was a heavy bag due to contents.

"I'm actually on my way back. I came through a few days ago with what ended up being a two thousand dollar investment and here's what I'm returning with."

Arthur opened and reached into the bag, pulling out a gold bar.

"This is a one-kilo gold bar. I have thirteen others in here. In the Twenty-First Century, each of these is worth close to forty thousand dollars. Our total investment is around eight to ten thousand dollars. Total value is well over a half a million in the Twenty-First Century. We buy the gold with the proceeds we get from the coin, notes, and stamps we sell. We re-smelt the gold in Key West, so there are no identification marks embossed on them. Then I take them back here on a time travel and sell them to the government. That's how we bought the building, your clothes, the wine and absinthe. It's just a matter of riding the right wave. We have our assistants to take care of and they get three percent of the net after the sale to the government here in 1922. They take care of the upkeep of the apartments and the like, plus, they live for free. It offers them a fabulous income and secures them for life. François is single, but if he marries, we will get him a larger flat in order to accommodate his wife and future family. This time period in Paris is one of our hubs that you landed in. There are others all over the world and in different times. We'll get into that in another conversation."

"Okay. How did François know to meet me in the toilet at Les Deux Magots?" Mark was full of logical questions.

"Great question!" Arthur said, smiling. "What day and time did you arrive there?"

"Today, at 10 am it looks like." Mark replied.

"Okay, just one second." He closed his eyes, held them closed for about thirty seconds, quivered a bit, he vanished and reappeared in less than a tenth of a second. Just a flash actually. Then he opened his eyes. "Done!"

"Done? What do you mean 'done'?"

"Well, I just time traveled to a week ago, informing François to meet you at Les Deux Magots with the appropriate things you would require at ten this morning and set up this room for you. Then I returned here. It was quite a trip." With a sigh, he pronounced "I've got to get to the government office with this, then to the bank. I'll be done by five if I get moving. By the way, I'm in number three on the second floor, if you should need me later."

With that François and Arthur finished their wine, then got up from the bar, bidding Mark adieu heading out the door.

This was incredible. There was more to learn. Mark knew he'd have to pick Arthur's brain. Meanwhile, he just felt gratitude. Being a time traveler wasn't a fluke after all, but rather a privilege and an honor. These people assisting him in the transition were so kind. Many questions still lingered of course. How did Arthur know he was coming to 1922, to begin with? Yes, he prepped François, but he was already here when he learned where and what time he landed. There was still a lot to learn, but he was excited to be learning more about the lifestyle he had somehow landed in. Here it was. He felt it actually *was* a society he had entered. And a society it surely was. The Organization of Time Travelers was actually a business, as well as a society. There was no question that they had time on their side. Enough information rendered for now, however.

On a related, albeit entirely different note, it was *April in Paris*.

Mark stepped out of his apartment building at 22 Rue de la Gare. It was six in the evening. What was he going to do? Where was he going to go? He was a slight bit hungry, and he knew it would intensify. He started walking in the direction of the popular areas in Paris, such as the Louvre, The Eiffel Tower and Notre Dame.

The evening temperature was becoming cooler, and he was glad he wore the corduroy jacket. After around twenty minutes of walking, his hunger started to intensify. There was a cafe on a corner that looked inviting. There was outside seating, but with the cool night air, he felt inside would be best. No point in tempting a 1922 cold, after all, he thought jokingly.

He greeted the maître d' just inside the door. The brasserie was bustling, and he was shown to a bench seat which extended down the wall, single tables spaced about a meter apart. His table was near the end, close to the bar. He had only given a quick look at the menu when the waiter arrived. A burgundy he ordered first, then continued perusing the menu, his standard procedure regarding libations and dinner. With the slight chill in the Spring air, something hearty might fit the requirements for a brisk evening. There was a potato with cheese and ham dish on the menu, Pommes de Terre Comtoises. That would stick to his ribs and fortify him against the chill of the evening. His wine arrived, and he submitted his order to the waiter who was very busy; he scampered off rapidly. There was no time for small talk tonight as he had with Marcel earlier at Les Deux Magots.

Mark leaned back to take in the busy establishment. He raised his glass, checking the nose of the burgundy. Meeting his approval, he took a sip as he canvassed the brasserie. That was when he saw it above the bar. It was a beautifully painted sign stretching across the back wall of the bar itself, which read La Closerie des Lilas.

How did he happen to end up here? Of all the thousands and thousands of cafes and brasseries in Paris, he just nonchalantly walks into the first cafe that strikes his interest, spurred on by a growling stomach, and he strolls into La Closerie des Lilas. It was one of the cafes which went down in history as a place where the literary groups would congregate.

His mouth dropped when he read the sign. "What the fuck!" he whispered to himself. An entirely twenty-first-century phrase, he realized it as soon as it slipped out.

"What's that sport?" The man sitting at the next table asked in English, with an American accent. It was very close proximity. So close, this man and woman sitting next to him were almost at the same table.

"Oh! Excuse me!" Mark apologized "I didn't mean that to be audible. I just wandered in here not knowing I was in La Closerie des Lilas. Of all the places in Paris, I'm here and don't realize this is where I ended up!"

The woman, seated right next to Mark, smiled.

The man continued, waving off Marks faux pas, "Think nothing of it! Well, where are you from old man?" He appeared to be in his mid-twenties, full of energy and what struck Mark as sincere interest.

"I'm from Key West. I came to Paris strictly on a recognizance mission of sorts," Mark exclaimed.

"Recognizance mission? Interesting, indeed! Key West?" The man asked in excitement, "That's the island out in the ocean, isn't that correct? You can take a train there, I believe?"

"That's the place!!" He felt he was going into the same conversation he had with Gertrude Stein earlier in the day. On the other hand, he was impressed that this fellow actually knew what Key West was. After all, he wasn't in Miami, or Tampa, he was in Paris, France, and this was 1922. The news didn't travel quite so fast here.

"Indeed, old sport! That's where the eighth wonder of the world is! The Seven Mile Bridge. Incredible! How long does it take to cross?"

"The bridge? About ten minutes. However, it's over fifty miles away from the mainland. There are over forty bridges the train crosses, hopping island to island. All in all, Key West is over one hundred miles out to sea."

"Zelda! Did you hear that?" he exclaimed.

"That's amazing, Scott! We'll have to go there one day!" Zelda replied. She had a distinctive but educated Southern accent.

Again, Mark's jaw dropped. "Wait a moment. Your names are Zelda and Scott?"

"Oh, I'm sorry, old man! I'm Scott and this is my wife Zelda. How do you do?" extending his hand.

"Fitzgerald?" Mark asked, half-puzzled.

Indeed. La Closerie des Lilas was yet another well-known spot for authors and artists alike. Picasso, Apollinaire, Hemingway, Fitzgerald, just to name a few, all came here. How did he wander into this establishment? Was it some sort of destiny? Is this a predetermined, surrealistic lifestyle? Was this the destiny of all time travelers?

He thought he was getting the feel for this time traveling life that was cast upon him. However, the more he did this, the more questions arose.

Scott reached over and gave his forearm a light shake. "Are you okay old sport? You look a little dazed."

"What? Old sport? The Great.... " Mark hesitated going further... he wondered if The Great Gatsby had been written yet? He didn't think so. It was 1922. Quickly thoughts raced through his mind. He remembered that This Side Of Paradise was his first success, and afforded him the ability to travel to, and live in Paris. Strictly fishing F. Scott Fitzgerald, he threw out the line.

"This Side Of Paradise is doing quite well I understand?"

"Oh, my! Is my book sold in Key West? That's truly incredible! I'm still getting used to the fact that my book is selling world wide! Honestly, I'm aghast!" He paused and took a breath, then continued, "It's done splendidly, thank you! I'm about to release my second, The Beautiful and the Damned, in a matter of days, actually. It has money, love, decadence of a society living in a nostalgic past. You don't know Gertrude Stein, by chance, do you?"

"Funny you mention her! I know her work and by chance, we actually met this morning. She invited me over for tomorrow's gathering."

"You don't say! Well, we'll be there as well! Is this your first time there?"

Suddenly, Zelda chimed in. "Gertrude's gatherings are a literary and artist gathering second to none. Well, almost none. There's one other in town, Shakespeare and Company, quite good really. Joyce actually uses Shakespeare and Company as his personal office!" she said laughing as she downed her glass of some mixed drink elixir.

She then turned to her husband "Scott, would you please get them to bring me another French 75?"

The French 75. Of course! Mark thought. It was served in a fluted champagne glass and named after a French artillery piece that gained fame in what this time period was known as "The Great War", though it's lineage went back further. The cocktail was a mix of brandy and champagne, with a helping of simple syrup and lemon juice. No wonder it was named after a French cannon! Zelda put the one she had down like a professional.

Scott spun around in his chair, spotting the waiter, busy across the room, hollering loudly while raising his hand "Rafael!!!" Then with two fingers raised when the waiter looked his way "Two more 75's! C'est vous plais. No! Make it three! One for our new friend!... Wait! Double for each! Six! Yes!" Then he repeated in French the number six. The waiter acknowledged saying "Tout de suite, Monsieur Fitzgerald!"

Scott spun back around and sat back in his chair. "I hope you don't mind me ordering you a couple of seventy-fives. They are on me, of course! Rafael knows just how to deliver them, too. He'll bring the three, then, seven minutes later, the other three will arrive, right as we're finishing the first ones. The second attack, as I call them. They are named after a French artillery piece, after all, arrives fresh and completely chilled to perfection. Oh! So you say you were with Gertrude earlier today?"

"Yes, we actually sat at the same table" Mark replied.

"You don't say? Splendid! Talking with Gertrude one-on-one is always an education. As I mentioned, we'll be there tomorrow night as well. You'll have a grand time, I have no doubt!"

They exchanged talk about Gertrude Stein's salon, as well as Key West and Mark's upbringing in Connecticut for a couple of minutes, when the waiter arrived with the fresh seventy-fives.

Mark, having been a bartender for quite a while, exclaimed, "For such a busy night, these drinks arrived very quickly."

"The staff knows I make it worth their while, old man! And, after all, who wants to keep Zelda waiting?" Scott replied, laughing.

It was an atmosphere of laughter and gaiety as the night progressed. The French 75's continued arriving, quite like the artillery barrage that was the source of their namesake. Mark had hit it off with Scott and Zelda Fitzgerald quite well. Here he was, getting entirely plastered with them.

Mark pulled his Roskopf out of his pocket. It was 11:56. At this point, he realized he was really quite intoxicated.

"Hey old man, I think we're all a bit embalmed at this stage."

It was obvious to anyone within a thirty-foot radius that this trio had more than their share of French 75's. Loud and boisterous, with cheering and laughter throughout the evening, Scott was going up to people at different tables all night long, back-slapping, carrying on, and buying them French 75's. At their twin tables, they actually should have backed off the recoil fire two hours ago, but Rafael continued delivering the artillery. There were several 75's in all of their stomachs which had yet to travel into their systems. No doubt the shrapnel of the evening would continue taking its toll through the next day.

Accordingly, Scott ordered the cheque from Rafael and generously paid the tab for all before ordering an ample helping for Rafael and the bartender.

As they headed out, Scott had a chauffeur driven 1921 Renault Type JP Model 45 pull up for their ride home. It was type of old-style limousine where the chauffeur was outside, with no roof, while the passenger compartment in the rear was warm and isolated. Mark ventured to think in his twentieth-century mind "That poor mo-fo!" He curbed his thought from being vocal.

"So! How did you get here tonight?" Scott asked shaking Marks' hand.

"I walked here from my apartment."

"Walked? Where's your place?"

"22 Rue de la Gare."

"You can't walk that far. We're all fried to the hat, and then some. You might end up in the gutter not even halfway there. We'll give you a lift. Get in!"

Mark thanked him and after Zelda got in, Mark did as well, followed by their host Scott. Once in, Scott grabbed a voice tube which went to the chauffeur "Humbert, please take us to 22 Rue de la Gare first." The chauffeur nodded and waved, as the limousine pulled away from La Closerie des Lilas.

Once underway, the passenger compartment became toasty warm in its opulent decor of the time. As it turned out, the compartment had its own gas fueled heater. It was quite cozy on this cold night. The interior was a dark purple velvet trim with cream colored pleated leather seats. There was a small bar consisting of Courvoisier, Rémy Martin, and Hennessy cognacs, along with a bottle of Perrier and old fashioned glasses. Opulent was a fitting description. Had he not downed so many French 75's, one of the elite cognacs would have been the perfect fit to ward off the April evening chill. His guess was that it was about fifty-five degrees Fahrenheit or thirteen degrees in the local Celsius metric reading. Quite a drop from when he arrived in Paris that morning. As things went, he was not drinking anything for the ride home.

"Well, we certainly got zozzled tonight, didn't we?" Zelda said with more than a slur.

Mark nodded and agreed "Oh yeah, we certainly tied one on, alright. That Rafael had it in for us!" He got a kick out of some of the sayings he was hearing from what was a bygone era. "Zozzled." You couldn't beat that with a stick. Why hadn't the term stuck?

After about a five-minute ride, they arrived at 22 Rue de la Gare. Everyone bid each other a good night and expressed interest in meeting tomorrow at Gertrude Stein's salon.

Mark observed blue exhaust smoke trailing behind, as the limousine motored slowly up the street. There goes success, riding the crest of the wave. Mark thought. A chauffeured limousine on the streets of Paris, in the very early hours of a Friday night and Saturday morning. Not a care in the world for those two. The world was, indeed, their oyster.

He fumbled for his key, then entered the building, then his apartment. He realized at this point how plastered he was from this night out with his new, well-heeled society friends, Scott and Zelda.

It was time for bed. He had enough of everything for one day. A chance meeting with Gertrude Stein, at Les Deux Magots, of all places. Then getting an apartment handed to him. Arthur showing up unexpectedly and rewarding him with some much-needed explanations. That evening, another chance meeting, this time with F. Scott Fitzgerald and his wife Zelda for what could only be described as a happenstance, wild drunken night in the La Closerie des Lilas, which he somehow stumbled across. Coincidences? He was in no shape to ponder anything as the final volley of French 75s started landing and taking their toll.

Yes, it was indeed time for bed.

Mark woke up in the apartment comfortably buried in comforters. There was a chill in the room, as the fire had long gone out. He thought he'd just languish in bed a while. The curtain that separated the bed area from the living room was open. The clock showed it was just before ten, while the light shining through the window offered a beautiful day outside.

On the other hand, he wasn't feeling at the top of his game. As a matter of fact, he was experiencing a serious misfire in his brain. No doubt, the results of uncountable French 75's that Rafael the waiter continued to bring the previous evening, crediting everyone to Scott's tab. Scott thought nothing of it. It was at his instruction after all. It had been a wild, crazy night, no argument there. Who could imagine? Somehow ending up at La Closerie des Lilas, being seated right next to, of all people, F. Scott Fitzgerald and his wife Zelda. Then, getting thoroughly trashed with them on an endless supply of French 75's high-ordnance cocktails.

He opened the armoire and picked out some suitable clothing for the morning. Perhaps he would knock on Arthur's door and see if he'd like to get a crème. This would be a good idea. After all, the last time he was with Arthur was riding bicycles and up Margaret Street in Key West, and jumping from 1935 to their natural 21st Century time. Stepping out, locking his door, Mark proceeded across the hall and knocked on Arthur's door.

Arthur greeted him warmly. He'd obviously been up for a bit and invited him in.

"You know? I think this may very well be the first time you've purposely come to see me."

"Ha ha! You may be right! Progress! Hey, would you care to grab a coffee with me? I could use one! Really crazy night last night!"

"Really? You'll have to fill me in! Coffee? Great idea! Can you give me five minutes? I need to run something quick by you as well. Your timing couldn't be better, actually."

"Sure! What's up?"

Arthur waved for Mark to follow him and lead him to his desk against the wall. His apartment was actually much like Mark's, albeit with everything in different locations.

Immediately, Mark noticed two identical satchels on the desk. One had to be the same satchel Arthur had yesterday at Mark's apartment.

"You'll be heading back to Key West 1935 tonight, then off to your standard time after a bit there." He grabbed one of the satchels and handed it to Mark. "The time has come where you can help support what we do. Bring this bag back to your time period. It's packed with coins, bills, and a few what we will call, antiques, by the time they get to our time."

The bag weighed around fifteen pounds.

"I'd better put it back in my room under lock and key. Anything else?"

"Yes, be certain it's secure, please. That's it. I'll head out with you. There's a quaint cafe just a block away we can go for that coffee," Arthur suggested.

They dropped off the satchel and headed to the cafe. On their arrival, the maître d' showed them to a table, followed by the waiter who took their order.

"You say I'm heading back tonight?" Mark inquired.

"Yes, don't forget, I came back from the future," Arthur said with a chuckle.

The coffees arrived and it was almost like taking a sacrament. The high octane of the espresso in the créme did wonders in lifting the fog that had been slowing Mark's brain. Arthur gave Mark the directions as to where to bring the bag when he arrived back in the twenty-first century. It actually wasn't in Key West but on the island before it, Stock Island. They chatted further and Mark brought Arthur up to date on this 1922 escapade and why he was doing it.

"You were smart to come back to 1922. By coincidence, we have one of our main points set up here, as you've seen. We have others. You'll visit them in time, no pun intended," Arthur said smirking.

This was yet another mystery that Mark found perplexing. How did he pick this year and this location? Here he was, doing research, and ending up in one of the hubs where time travelers generate their revenue. He didn't have time to ponder it further now. He'd address it on another date.

They both laughed and finished up. Arthur was heading to the Louvre while Mark thought it best to catch a bit more rest before heading to Gertrude Stein's salon later. He headed back to the apartment and stretching out on the bed was his first order of business. The sun was coming in through the window and the apartment was warm. No need for the fire to be rekindled now. It was around half past noon and he dozed off quickly.

He fell into a long, deep sleep and was awoken by the grandfather clock chiming. It was 4:00, so he had plenty of time to get to Gertrude's salon.

The bathroom was on the diagonal from the bedroom, in the corner across the living room. He drew a bath, got in and lounged in it for a while, just taking it all in. Tubs like this weren't made anymore. There was no doubt about that. The tub had four legs, one on each corner and each looking like a lion's paw. The spigot looked like a lion's head and, as you would expect, the water came out of its mouth. It was quite like the type of a town fountain, found in European countries such as France, Spain, Portugal, or Italy. He was, however, grateful that it wasn't a reproduction of the Belgian statue, Manneken Pis.

After his bath, he went to the armoire and picked out some appropriate attire for the salon. He realized at this point that his new friends, Scott and Zelda, were actually dressed to the nines last evening. If this was a guide to how people were dressed for the salon, he took that as his cue.

He headed over to 27 Rue de la Fleures, the home of Gertrude Stein and her life partner Alice B. Toklas. He arrived a tad early, maybe ten minutes ahead of time. It was Alice who answered the door. She

146

was wearing an apron and it was clear that she was working in the kitchen at the time. Mark introduced himself saying that Miss Stein had invited him yesterday.

Alice laughed and said "Oh yes! She told me a gentleman from an exotic island off the United States was coming today! Please come in. My name is Alice. Follow me. I'll steer you in the right direction for Gertrude, however, I do have things to attend to in the kitchen which I need to get back to. Are you an artist, or an author?"

"Actually, I'm a fan of both. My profession is that of a bartender," Mark replied.

"Interesting. So, the reality is that you're a psychologist!" Alice stated jokingly.

They both laughed, then Mark replied: "That's actually one of many hats bartenders have to wear!"

Mark followed her through the foyer and into a living room. There were paintings all over the walls. It wasn't as though any were allowed to breathe on a wall of their own. All were packed almost as many as could fit on the wall. It was a lot like walking into the antique store in Key West, and others like it, where items would be all over the place and one had to make their way around them. However, here the pieces were hanging on the wall. Additionally, the ceiling was very high, over ten feet, perhaps twelve. The pieces went from the top of the walls to the top of the furniture.

Fascinating pieces, every one, however! And what artists! Damn it, there were a few Picasso pieces up there! There was a Matisse... and a Renoir, a Manet, a Gauguin. Mark realized that, in his time, the room he was standing in was worth easily over one hundred million dollars. Perhaps double that. All of these works, hanging haphazardly, almost in a wallpaper fashion, covering as much of the wall as possible. It was honestly just incredible. Alice excused herself while Mark continued looking at the pieces in total amazement. He was the only one in the room. No one else had arrived at this point. He felt he was in a museum, or was it a storage shed for masterpieces? Either way, this was a room that was just seeping greatness from the walls themselves.

Suddenly Gertrude burst into the room walking at a brisk pace, greeting Mark with an extended hand.

"Mark! I'm so glad you could make it. You're the first one here, actually. I'm surprised. I thought you might be on the notorious island time, coming from Key West? Interestingly, I'll say one would think artists and authors came from exotic tropical islands; they are seldom on time for anything! I've found that if it's a pressing issue and you require them to be someplace at say, five, tell them anywhere between four and four-thirty, depending on the individual and their habits."

Mark gave a light laugh, but Gertrude wasn't laughing, or even smiling for that matter. She impressed Mark as being a direct and to the point type of individual.This was, however, the way she delivered her slant on humor. She struck him as being very organized. On the other hand, there was the disorganization of all the artwork on the walls. This belied the first thought, almost like sugar dissolving in a cup a tea. Yet, the first thought of her being organized seemed embedded in concrete. Miss Stein was certainly the walking, talking definition of an enigma. There was no doubt about that, at least at this stage. This was in no way a negative perception of

Mark's, but rather one of awe and fascination. The left side of her brain did certain things, while the right did the others.

"I must confess, Miss Stein. I'm usually on island time. The bar I work at in Key West is called 'The Side Car'. It's a running joke that I'll consistently roll in for work five to ten minutes late. However, having the honor bestowed on me to be your guest here today, I made certain I was on time."

"That's refreshing to hear, and likewise, experience someone being on time for once. Also, it's just Gertrude. We'll have none of this 'Miss Stein' from this point forward."

When she said Miss Stein, she raised both of her arms and with her fingers made the sign for a quote. There was a very, very slight smirk that went with it. Mark realized that this was as far as her sense of humor extended. He also picked up that Gertrude only allowed this bit of mirth to be seen by a select few.

"Gertrude it is then," Mark said, nodding and shaking her hand and looking directly into her eyes while doing so. She was an intense personality and the eye-to-eye contact was something that made an impression on her. Someone who would look away didn't have the focus or passion for their quests in life. Gertrude fed off of other people's passions, as they did with her. Someone who didn't look her directly in the eye lacked the focus and passion in life that she fed off of and from their point, they found Gertrude overwhelming.

"Mark, I'm not going to beat around the bush, but rather hit the nail directly on the head. I'm good at reading people. Not meaning to boast, just speaking matter of fact, I have yet to meet anyone who is on the same playing field as myself. When I met you at the cafe, I was taken in with you. You are someone like no other that I've ever met. There is something very different about you. I can't put my finger on it. You're different, really different. Now, I also know that you're sincere, honest as the day is long, and have a solid character. That I picked up from the start. Now, I don't pick up anything negative at all, but I also sense that you know exactly what I'm talking about, don't you?"

In a certain way, it almost seemed, with her compliments, that Gertrude was coming onto him. However, that was only a brief surface impression, and just for a hint of an instant. Only a lesser person would have allowed that thought to linger. That wasn't Mark, though. He knew exactly what she was seeing in him, that she couldn't put a finger on. He, of course, knew what it was. He also felt comfortable with her. Very comfortable. As a matter of fact, it was as though she was somewhere between an older sister and a maternal figure.

"Gertrude, I must say I feel as though I'm almost related to you. I felt this way at the cafe when we were introduced. Can we sit down in private? I know precisely what you're talking about. I'd like to explain it to you privately and in strict confidence."

Gertrude thought for a second after Mark told her this. They never lost direct eye contact.

In her matter of fact demeanor, she nodded, "Yes, follow me."

She directed him to an archway, which headed into another room. From there, a curtain which separated a smaller room, which obviously was her office. Gertrude pulled the curtain aside, and they entered. Like the other room, both the archway room and this office sized room were covered in art pieces, wallpapering the walls.

There was a desk and a settee in front of it. Gertrude pointed to the settee. "Make yourself comfortable. I must admit, you have my curiosity peaked. I've known artists, poets, authors, and musicians. Frankly, I get all of them within a conversation. I get a lot of you, but there's this one part that's totally a blank mystery," she said as she sat in a large, comfortable looking chair.

"Gertrude, what I'm going to tell you will most likely be met with common sense. Your brain will be telling you that I must be either out of my mind or on some kind of opiates. I assure that I am of complete sound mind."

Gertrude's head cocked to the side, then straightened out and in her direct way replied "Okay, go ahead."

Mark took a long breath then started slowly "Gertrude…" he paused for about five seconds, then took a deep breath and continued, again very slowly "I am not from this time. Right now, it's 1922, correct?"

Gertrude had a puzzled look on her face as her head instinctively pulled back a few inches upon hearing this. "Yes, it's Saturday, the 22nd of April, 1922."

"Well, the fact of this all is, I won't be born for almost sixty years. Gertrude, I'm a time traveler. When I met you the other day, I had just come from another time travel from 1935. I had been in a bar in Key West and met Ernest Hemingway. He recognized me to a slight degree. Of course, I hadn't met him as I didn't do that time travel yet. So, I excused myself, went to the men's room, where I time jumped to Les Deux Magots thirteen years in arrears and 4,700 miles. Just after my arrival, I met you because of my waiter there, Marcel."

"You're right, this is hard to fathom. You know Ernest Hemingway? That kid has so much potential. I think he should drop the magazine and newspaper writing, poetry as well, and become a novelist. That's where he should be heading. He'll be here today," Gertrude replied while rubbing her forehead in the bewilderment of it all. "Time traveler? I don't know what to say about that."

"Trust me please on that, Gertrude. As far as Hemingway goes, just don't stop what you're doing with him."

"This time travel is something I'm having trouble understanding. It just can't be real. I'm sorry. It's perplexing because I know you are an honest man. It's a clear paradox." She paused and neither said anything for about fifteen uncomfortable seconds. Gertrude then broke that ice she created by asking, "So you know Ernest?"

"I've met him. I can't say I know him. Listen, I have an idea. Do you trust me?"

"I do."

"Do you want to see a small portion of the future?"

"How is that Mark?"

"Good. Take hold of my forearm and close your eyes."

Gertrude paused, then a bit cautiously put her hand on Mark's forearm across the desk. He closed his eyes and concentrated on going back to his own time. He'd been away for a while, after all. Additionally, he had the perfect location to go to with Gertrude.

"Keep your eyes closed Gertrude. Trust me, please. You'll feel a bit dizzy, but just trust me on this please."

The room started spinning and they both felt as though they were tumbling in weightlessness. After a few seconds, they were sitting in a beautiful tropical garden, on a bench seat with a path leading to it with a lot of tropical foliage. It was a stunning day as well, about eighty degrees.

There was a two story beautiful home, in a French style, with a wide, wrap around balcony on the second story.

Mark looked at Gertrude, who was clearly in awe and bewilderment.

"Mark, where are we? How did we get here? What the heck is going on? How did we leave my office?"

"Gertrude, you are now in my natural time. It's the twenty-first-century and I'm glad you're sitting down because you are now in Key West, The place you're sitting in is the garden of Ernest Hemingway's home."

"This is Hemingway's home? Is he in? I want to see him."

"I'm afraid in this time period, he's been dead for around sixty years, give or take. But this is his home. He moved here from Paris. Let's take a look around."

"It's such a large house, how did he afford it?"

"Gertrude, we should take a tour. They have them every half hour I believe."

They walked to the front of the house and there was a tour gathering which they latched onto. The guide was a man who called himself "Boston Bob". The tour lasted around a half hour and, throughout it, Gertrude would look at Mark with a very inquisitive look. The tour was handled very well, informative and an educational guide through the house and grounds, filled with history about Hemingway's life, most of which was about his life living in Key West. For Hemingway, that started in 1929, seven years after the time travel jump to Paris. "Apparently, Ernest made quite a name for himself," Gertrude was thinking. The look she gave Mark when Boston Bob referred to Hemingway as "Perhaps America's most prolific author" was best described as awe.

Mark couldn't help smiling when they were on the second floor and Gertrude saw over and beyond the brick wall surrounding the house. She looked quite bewildered at the cars as they drove by on Whitehead Street! Inside the property, there really wasn't much of a difference between, say 1922 and Mark's twenty-first century time period. However, seeing twenty-first-century cars driving by was paramount. Gertrude's jaw had literally dropped when this came into view for her.

At the end of the tour, Mark brought her to the bookstore, just off the grandiose pool, which Boston Bob had a very funny anecdote about, focussed around, of all things, a penny.

Inside the bookstore was crowded with people from all over the world. It was tiny as well, Gertrude's eyes lit up at all the books

Hemingway had written and marveled at the titles. *A Farewell to Arms, For Whom The Bell Tolls, Death In The Afternoon, To Have and Have Not, The Green Hills of Africa, Islands In The Stream, The Sun Also Rises*. She was in complete amazement. She flipped through several books in complete awe.

Meanwhile, Mark found he still had some money in his wallet that was both American and from his era. He purchased a book. Then approached Gertrude from behind and while putting a reassuring hand on her shoulder said, "Gertrude, it's vitally important that you continue to support Hemingway the way you've been doing. Don't deviate at all. Just keep doing what you've been doing. If you do, he will become what many consider America's greatest author. Don't do any more, or any less. You and he will naturally have your ups and downs, but persevere! Things will fall into place."

"There are so many books he's written! This is his forte. I keep saying he's wasting his time with the newspapers and magazines. So he is a well-known author in this time."

"Gertrude, millions, and millions will champion Hemingway as America's finest author. Not just Americans either. I'm talking the world over."

He then headed her back to the bench in the garden. They sat down and Mark said "You have guests coming in 1922 to your salon. We should head back." Gertrude nodded and again, put her hand back on his forearm.

Next thing, they were back in her office, her in the chair behind the desk and Mark in the settee, her hand on his forearm. Again, the dizziness was there but faded quickly. She looked at the clock and it was the same time as to when they left.

"We were gone for at least forty minutes, yet it's the same time it was when we left! I don't get it."

"With time traveling one can do this, Gertrude. And believe me, I have a LOT to learn about it still."

"Time traveling. If I didn't experience it myself, I'd never have believed it! And those automobiles I saw. They looked like they were from another planet! I am totally aghast!" Gertrude gasped as she collected her lost breath. Additionally, her eyes were tearing.

This was the first time Gertrude expressed real emotion that he had seen. He had a feeling that this was indeed an isolated incident.

"Gather yourself up, Gertrude. Guests will be arriving any minute."

"Please don't mention my emotional state..."

"Of course not, Gertrude. We have each other's trust and bond."

"Indeed, we do. Before, I couldn't say why I invited you. After all, we only spent at most, an hour together at Les Deux Magots over a crème or two. Honestly, I'm very reserved as to whom I invite to the salon. As I said earlier, I knew there was *something* about you that I couldn't put my finger on. I'm very thankful I invited you and grateful that you came Mark. You have a quirky way about you that fits right in here perfectly. We have artists, writers, poets, musicians and now, the big hidden secret, a time traveler!" She was smiling ear to ear at this point. Something not taken lightly by Mark, as he well knew her reputation as one who was largely taken to be quite stoic. She rose from her chair behind the desk.

"Before we head to the gathering in the other room," Mark interceded, "There's one last thing. This must be stashed away, never to be seen by anyone but yourself for as long as you live, plus, no one can ever know about it." He then handed her a book he had purchased. It was a copy of *A Farewell To Arms*. "This book won't be written and published for another seven years. Additionally, if you look at the date inside the book, it reads 'Copyright 1929' Renewed 2016'. However, it's a little memento of our voyage today that you will always have".

"I assure you, Mark, this shall be secured. Thank you very much for such an experience today. I can honestly say that it's something that I will take to the grave with me." She then took the book to the bookshelf behind her and pulled two books out. She then put A Farewell To Arms behind them. "I really am looking forward to reading this, I must say! When I stop and think about, I've never read a book prior to its writing!"

They alighted from the office and into the room with the arch, where people were gathering in the main living room. As they entered through the archway, others were entering through the main entrance.

The first was a man wearing a beret. He threw his arms around Gertrude, kissing her on both cheeks and saying in distinctive Castilian Spanish, "Ah! Hertrud, mi amor, que pasa?"

Mark easily was able to discern the accent from Spain from that of the Cubans in Key West. It sounded as though the back of their tongue was locked to their upper molars when they spoke, additionally, the "s" in the word "paso" was almost pronounced like an English "th". He also pronounced the G in her name like an H. This Spanish use would be the same in the Cuban dialect, of which he was more familiar. It stood out, however, as this was the first time he heard it.

No doubt about it. This was Pablo Picasso.

Gertrude turned and introduced Pablo to Mark, then turned back to greet other guests who were arriving. Mark, having seen Picasso's work, both before and after this moment in 1922, engaged in conversation with the artist regarding Cubist art which, of course, Picasso was always credited as a co-founder. The conversation was in a combination of French and Spanish. Mark's French was better than his Spanish. Fortunately, Picasso spoke both.

Mark inquired about his name. Picasso, of course, was his name and he was completely and entirely a Spaniard. Of that, there was no doubt. However, the double s in his surname made it Italian, not Spanish. Pablo explained that his mother was one-quarter Italian, and that part of her family originated in Genoa, Italy. Laughing, he stated that "Colon also hailed from Genoa! Only the finest Italians came to Spain from Genoa!"

Mark felt a little lost here, not to mention embarrassed. Who was Colon? Being a DJ and from the New York metropolitan area, he, of course, knew of Willie Colon, the New York born salsa musician of Puerto Rican heritage. However, he wouldn't be born for another two generations. Who was Picasso be talking about?

He asked him, "Colon?"

158

Picasso looked at him in astonishment and exclaimed, "Si! Colon! You know Colon!"

Mark looked bewildered at him. Picasso astonished with his arms flailing in the best of Latin expression, blurted out, "Si! Colon! Cristobal Colon!".

At this point, Gertrude saw the situation and came to the rescue. Switching the language to French from Spanish, as the latter part had been, she stepped in, to their aid.

"Oh, Pablo! This is one of the funniest things!" She said laughing.

Laughing, yes laughing. Gertrude Stein was laughing *twice* in one day. If they took bets on this in Monte Carlo, down on the French Riviera, no one of sane mind would ever bet Gertrude would laugh once a year, never mind twice in one day! The bank would collapse, without question! Apparently, this was a threat that a new precedent was at hand!

"Pablo, for reasons I cannot explain why, that unfortunate man has a different name in every language! In Spanish, it's Cristobal Colon. In Italy where he was born and actually christened, it's Cristoforo Columbo, in French it's Christophe Colomb, and in English, for Mark's benefit, it's Christopher Columbus!"

"Oh! Columbus! I feel like such an ass!" Mark exclaimed.

Picasso laughed hardheartedly as well. "Such confusion! All have a different name for the fellow. We all want to claim him as our own!"

At this point, there was quite a crowd gathered. Mark took the initiative, noticing all had a glass of wine in their hand, he raised his high and took the floor by storm.

"A toast to Cristoforo Columbo, Cristobal Colon, Christophe Colomb, and Christopher Columbus!"

The whole group, lighthearted and jovial, hoisted their glassed in toast, hollering their toast in their native tongues, with unadulterated enthusiasm!

"Salud!" "Cheers!" "Chin-Chin!" "Gesundheit!" "Salute!" "Nastrovie!"

As Mark was taking his second sip after the toast, Gertrude was back suddenly.

"Mark! I wanted you to meet this young man, also from the States, Ernest Hemingway." Then turning back to a young man in his early twenties saying "Ernest, I'd like to introduce you to Mr. Mark Straight. He's from Key West. Mark, Ernest is a fine writer. I feel he has a *lot* of potential."

"How do you do, Mr. Straight? My name is Ernest and this is my wife, Hadley."

"How do you do, Ernest. Hadley." Then, adding to the cloak of feigned lack of knowledge of the young man of twenty-three, when he actually knew him like a book, "What brings you to Paris and what do you do?"

"I'm a foreign correspondent for the Toronto Star. Hadley and I were married last year. The job landed us in Paris, where I had several letters of introduction. Actually, we had Rome as our first choice destination. We love Paris thus far, plus we've met so many fascinating people, such as Miss Stein. We're so very glad to be here. Fate having us land here was a Godsend."

"Miss Stein has your best interests in heart and she's *the* Grande Dame sage of the past, present, and things to come. If you'd care for a suggestion?"

"By all means. Speak your mind." For a young man of twenty-three talking to a man who was sixteen years his senior, yet unknowingly actually over eighty years his junior, Hemingway was very direct and not intimidated whatsoever.

"In your shoes Ernest, I'd take Gertrude Stein's advice very seriously. She's been around a lot of different blocks in this town over the years. There's no substitute for experience. She has it, Ernest."

Ernest looked at him directly in the eyes. Mark never wavered from Hemingway's stare which lasted a good five seconds. It was almost akin to a challenge.

"You're an honest and sincere man, Mr. Straight. I see you mean what you say. A lesser man would have looked away, had he been insecure about his statement. Cheers." Hemingway raised his glass of red wine.

Mark said nothing, never losing his stare, raising his glass and returning the toast with a perfunctory, single nod. Then, after a pause, Mark stated: "Not Mr. Straight, Ernest. Just Mark, please."

"Very well, Mark. Here, let's move into the adjoining room. Alice is about to serve dinner. She's quite the chef. She is particular regarding seating arrangements. However, between you and me, she isn't all that concerned regarding writers. It's the painters she's more concerned about. Can you keep a secret?"

"Of course. A secret between two ex-patriots in Paris. A better bond could not be found."

"Her secret is placing the artists looking at their own paintings! That keeps them happy as clams looking at their own work hanging on someone else's wall!" Hemingway laughed without restraint.

He then walked over to Alice B. Toklas and struck up a brief conversation. After a minute he returned to Mark and Hadley. There would be no problem with Mark and Ernest sitting across from one another, Ernest cleared the path with Alice. A formality, yet a necessary one in the protocol of the house. Hadley was sitting to Ernest's right. As it turned out, there was an Irishman sitting next to his left.

He was a pale fellow with glasses. He had been talking to a man in English, prior to sitting down. That was how Mark noticed his Dublin derived brogue. The Irishman then turned to another man speaking to him in Italian. Next, he spoke to a beautiful blond woman in a Scandinavian language. Mark was guessing it was a western dialect of Norwegian, however, that was but a guess. He was sure it wasn't Danish, and definitely not Swedish. Icelandic would never cross his mind after hearing it. When he sat down, he greeted Ernest in English shaking his hand, then nodded at Mark extending his hand saying, "Bonsoir. Je m'appelle James". He introduced himself in French, using the English pronunciation of his name, James.

Mark extended his hand across the table. "James? I heard what I thought was a Dublin accent? If so and if you don't mind, my English is better than my French."

Ernest suddenly burst in. "Oh, James speaks English better than a Londoner, or at least as good as the best!"

Mark smiled, shaking James' hand. "How do you do James? My name is Mark Straight."

"James Joyce. Straight? Ha! We have a bunch of Straights in Ireland and also Straits and Straitons as well. They are all connected and share lineage with family in Scotland with the same names. It's a lot like whiskey. The Scottish arm says the clan originated there, while the Irish say the clan originates from The Emerald Isle. Now, while your name is Strait, your Yank accent suggests that they may only be distant relatives?"

"We're more Irish than Scottish, however the family itself is always at odds regarding the family heritage, just as you say!" He then continued after James smiled and, nodding approvingly, inquired, "James Joyce? The author?"

"Yes, my boy, that would be me. A striving author and a hungry one at that. Only wishing to keep a roof over my head, is all I ask".

Mark's memory went back for but a flash, to Captain Tony's only a day and a half ago, and thirteen years in the future, when he thought

Hemingway was talking about a woman when he mentioned Joyce by his last name only. He smiled at the thought.

Hemingway then added in awe, "He is releasing his latest work in a matter of days, *Ulysses*. It's one of the best pieces of literature I've ever read!"

About this time Mark realized that he was sitting at a table in 1922 Paris with Ernest Hemingway and James Joyce. Pablo Picasso was only a few seats down. Gertrude Stein was at the head of the table, while Alice B, Toklas was serving a gourmet dinner of Boeuf Bourguignon.

Suddenly, fashionably late, in strolled F.Scott Fitzgerald and his wife Zelda. They stopped to say hello to Mark, prior to Alice leading them to the other end of the banquet table.

"Hello, Mark! How are you feeling today?" Scott inquired as Alice lead him past.

"Okay now, but earlier I felt like cannon fodder from the seventy-fives".

Everyone at the table laughed. Apparently, Mark wasn't the only one to be on the receiving end of Scott and Zelda's volley of French seventy-five salvos.

After the laughter died down, Hemingway asked Mark ,"Where in the States are you from?"

"I'm from Key West. It's an island off the tip of Florida. It's actually closer to Cuba than the mainland of Florida."

"I've heard of it. Dos Passos has mentioned it to me. Sounds like an interesting place actually".

After this Ernest and James took to talking writing, writers, and their styles, in addition to the best strong points particular writers had. Mark found it all quite fascinating. How often do you get to be a fly on the wall listening to a conversation between Ernest Hemingway and James Joyce? Seriously? Unbelievable! Every now and then, one or the other would bring Mark or Hadley into the conversation with a question. Each would answer the question proposed, then everyone would talk about it for a minute or two. Ernest and James would continue then on their various writing conversations for as long as it took, as not to be rude, at which point they'd bring Hadley and Mark back into the conversation again by asking one of them a question. They were very polite in doing so, and this was not lost on Mark.

At the end of the evening, Mark said goodnight to everyone he met. Ernest and Hadley, James Joyce, Picasso, Scott and Zelda, Alice, then finally Gertrude, whom he told he was off on a trip and wasn't sure when he'd be back. "Stay on Ernest's back about doing the right thing for him." He then paused saying with a direct look and a nod. "I know you will."

"Thank you, Mark, for that amazing experience. It's something I will never forget my entire life," Gertrude replied as she grabbed Mark's forearms firmly. They gave each other the customary two kisses, one on each cheek, and he headed for the door.

Ernest was now talking to someone whom Mark never got to meet right near the front door. As Mark passed he patted Ernest on the back saying "Great meeting you. Remember my advice regarding Gertrude. We will meet again, though I'm not sure when." Ernest smiled and nodded as Mark passed.

Suddenly, Mark stopped and pulled out his iPhone and snapped around a dozen pictures of everyone. They all looked puzzled. He smiled and gave a friendly wave. He was out the door in a heartbeat, before anyone could ask what he was doing.

The evening temperature was cool. He walked along the streets of Paris, just admiring it's nocturnal beauty with every step. He made sure to take additional pictures on his way home. Meanwhile, the thought of the entire visit was going through his head like a freight train that refused to stop.

When he got to his room, he was exhausted. He laid on the bed and promptly fell asleep. It was a very deep sleep. A sleep that was well earned. When he woke up, it was after eight in the morning. Getting up, he found a note on the table from Arthur. He had to go back and would see Mark later, in his regular time. Damn. Mark realized he was supposed to leave last night. Would this mean anything?

He headed out to the same cafe he and Arthur went to the day before. It was a beautiful morning. Mark had a crème and two croissants, then headed back to his apartment.

He went in and looked at the bag he would be taking back with him. He opened it up. Everything seemed in order. He reached into his pocket and left several hundred francs for Francois on the bar.

Grabbing the bag, he closed his eyes, and concentrated on Key West, 1935, the day, and minute that he left.

He again felt the lightheaded, and weightless, tumbling feeling that occurred when he would be time traveling.

Suddenly he was in the bathroom at Sloppy Joe's and the drunk was laying on the floor looking at him in amazement.

The drunk suddenly blurted out "Hey! What the hell? You just vanished into thin are for a few seconds and then you reappeared!"

"Only three seconds? That's fantastic! I got there Friday morning, spent Friday, Saturday, and Sunday morning in Paris and now I'm back in only three seconds! That's incredible!"

"What? Paris? Friday, Saturday, and Sunday? What are you talking about?"

Mark figured the best thing to do here was just keep him confused.

"Look, Bub, you say I came in here and vanished into thin air for three seconds then reappeared. Well, look at yourself. You're lying on the floor of the men's room at Sloppy Joe's. Think about what you said pal. What would you expect me to tell you? Vanished? You know, this bar has a great selection of Cuban Rum. Why don't you go have yourself another shot?"

One never knows?

He left the poor drunk grumbling and headed back to the bar. Glades and Ernest were having a jovial chat at the bar, now joined by Josie. He set the satchel at the base of the bar. No one noticed.

"Josie! Meet Mark! He's a bartender over at The Victoria Restaurant."

"How do you do Mark? I'm Josie Russell. The Victoria? Nice place indeed with a very good menu. A good place to work I'm told," Josie said, extending his hand.

"Nice to meet you, Josie, I'm Mark Straight. Yes, the Victoria is a great restaurant with a great staff," nodding to Glades. Everyone laughed.

"You know Ernest? I think I may have met you in Paris, 1922. I was there on a trip and met a young writer at Gertrude Stein's. She was pushing him to move from magazines to literature. Could that have been you?"

Ernest laughed "Indeed it was! I think I recall that evening, now that you mention it. It was at her salon and I think my first wife Hadley and I may have been seated with you for dinner. If so, I recall your advice was to listen to Gertrude."

"Yes, that was me alright."

"Gertrude! She's a ticket alright. We've had our ups and downs, but we both have strong personalities, so that's inevitable. She's a good woman, however, and attracts the most interesting people to her home. No doubt about that."

At the end of that sentence, the drunk in the bathroom staggered by. He leaned to Hemingway and said, "That guy you're talking to is some kind of magician. He knows how to disappear into thin air!"

"You don't say?" Hemingway replied, a bit taken aback, then continued "Look here Eddie, I'm going to let you in on a little secret. You're the inspiration for a character in my story *One Trip Across,* which appeared in Cosmopolitan last year. Eddie was the rummy deck hand of the protagonist, Harry Morgan. This disappearing act just wouldn't fly though. I think you need to take a break from the sauce, Eddie."

"Really! I'm not kidding! He did disappear, Ernest. Right in front of my eyes! Then a few seconds later, reappeared. Said he went on a three-day trip or something? New York, Rome... someplace."

Ernest put his arm around Eddie and lead him to the door. "You've had enough for one day, Eddie. Head home and sleep it off."

Eddie headed out the door nodding his head.

Ernest returned to the group at the bar.

"That Eddie is one heck of a rummy alright. Seeing you disappear. What? Are you doing a Houdini act and the men's room of Sloppy Joe's is your rehearsal studio?"

Everyone roared a collective, jovial outburst. They talked about bartending, fishing, drinking but, out of respect for Glades, the subject of women was sidestepped. Ernest and Josie went on for a good while telling fishing tales and adventures out on the water. Hemingway turned to Mark and stated firmly, albeit with a bit of alcohol inspiration, "You have to see my boat! Her name is Pilar and, as I mentioned earlier, it was built in New York. Thirty-seven feet, two engines, one is for trawling. Maybe you two can go out with Pauline and I for a little day cruise. Josie and his wife can come, too. We'll make a picnic out of it. Bring some sandwiches and beer. Sound good to you?"

Glades, with a broad, excited smile on her face asked, "Really?"

"Of course! I don't say things lightly. Let's do it!"

Going out with Hemingway on his boat Pilar. What next? Of course, he would agree to the idea!

"Sounds great to me. When?"

Talk about a wild experience.

"Tomorrow at one in the afternoon. I'm busy with writing in the morning each day. If that works for you, one o'clock is good for me. You know where I live. Meet me at my house and we'll drive over to the boat in my Ford."

"Is it possible that we could be back by four? Glades and I are working tonight," Mark inquired.

"That's not a problem at all" Hemingway replied. "Pauline has a three-hour tolerance for being out on the boat most of the time."

"That sounds excellent! Thank you for inviting us!" Mark replied, extending his hand to shake Hemingway's.

Hemingway had a strong, firm handshake. It was a handshake with a long background of muscles exercised in typing words, pulling triggers, and reeling fishing reels. It was what Mark expected and he wasn't let down.

Everyone bid each other farewell and all seemed excited about the next day's excursion into the waters off Key West.

Mark turned to Glades. "I have a few errands to run. Can I meet you at your place at six?"

"I have a few things I have to do as well. I have to head to Fausto's Grocery for one. I'll make dinner. See you at six" She said, then gave him a kiss and headed out.

It went a little easier than he'd been expecting. He was concerned she would see the satchel, which he didn't have earlier when they arrived. It wasn't as though he had stuck it in his pocket, after all.

That was his first responsibility. He paid his tab, then headed back into the men's room.

He was off and traveling to his current time to take care of essential business.

In seconds he was back in his own time. It was still the bright, sunny morning he left to see Glades. That seemed so long ago! He jumped to Key West, 1935, from there to Paris, April 1922 where he stayed a few days, then back to Sloppy Joe's original bar, 1935 with Glades, Hemingway, Josie Russell, and Skinner. Frankly, he could use a rest. He put the satchel under his bed and stretched out for a few hours. It was a sound, deep sleep filled with dreams he could not remember upon awakening. He checked the time. 12:37 pm.

He pulled the directions out of his pocket that Arthur gave him in Paris. The Stock Island location where he would deliver the satchel was in a warehouse area of town. In addition to the address, it also had a phone number and a name. The number started off with 305 296, so he knew it was a landline. The name on the paper was Steve Craig.

The paper was interesting unto itself. 1922 Parisian stationery. It was thick and had a musky air to it. Mark pulled out his phone and dialed the number. It rang several times, then a male voice answered. "Hello, Mark Straight! This is Steve Craig. Arthur told me you'd be calling this afternoon."

The voice and what went with it caught Mark a bit off guard, and he hesitated a moment. A bit off balance, he recoiled saying, "Geeze! You guys don't miss a fucking beat, do you?"

The voice of Steve Craig came back laughing, then saying "Not when it comes to our *fucking* finances! When do you think you'll get here?" He seemed like a fun individual on the phone. Fun, yet serious at the same time.

"I can be there in about an hour."

"Good! We'll see you at, say, 1:45."

"Perfect!"

Mark gathered himself up, grabbed a bite to eat and a shower. The Stock Island location was about six miles away, so he called a cab.

The warehouse was in an industrial part of the island. It certainly didn't look at all opulent. The buildings were all old and white, with a very weathered look, just a shade shy of being classified as "run down." He paid the cab and rang the bell at the door. The door opened and the gentleman proclaimed "Dr. Straight, I presume?" mimicking Henry Morton Stanley's 1871 greeting of David Livingstone on the shore of Lake Tanganyika in Africa. Funny, here it was almost one-hundred and fifty years later and the expression was still in use.

"Yes sir, I'm Mark Straight. You are, no doubt, Steve Craig?"

"Indeed I am! Please come in!" They shook hands and entered the facility.

Inside, the facility was quite different than the outside suggested. There was a small vestibule, with an additional door on the other side. The inside door was opulent, very heavy and secure, though when it swung open it was extremely well balanced and opened as though it were on ball bearings.

174

The reception area was furnished with the highest quality furniture. A desk with a phone and computer, with seating provisions for three guests. A door lead to the back.

"Let's go to the back! Follow me, Mark."

Steve Craig, as it turned out, was a retired gentleman, sporting gray hair in a pony tail. He had a youthful spring to his walk as he opened the door to the rear of the facility. In the back there was another office to start, then what appeared to be a foundry, along with two other rooms with their doors closed.

Steve lead the way into the office, holding the door open for Mark, then closing it behind him. He then motioned him to sit in one of the chairs at the desk while he circled around and sat facing him.

"Let's not beat around the bush, so to speak," Steve said laughing. "Pass me that satchel!"

Mark smiled and put the satchel on the table. Steve pulled everything out and laid it out neatly. He opened a drawer and pulled out a paper with an itemized list and he checked them off the list. After a few minutes, he finished and proclaimed "Everything is perfect, Mister Straight!

"This is your first delivery. There will be more naturally. It's an easy and fascinating profession that goes well with the completely surrealistic lifestyle of a time traveler."

"Are you a time traveler yourself?" Mark inquired.

"I am. However, like yourself, I have not been one all my life. None of us are actually. I'm sure Arthur explained that we're all impeccably honest, with a very high I.Q.s and ethics standards. These things aren't established until we're all adults with a long track record. None of us understand how becoming a time traveler comes about, but we're almost smart enough to figure it's our one common denominator!" Steve said laughing.

He continued saying "I'm not really sure how the next process will work, at least as far as you're concerned. We have a few of these style investments scattered around the country and the world. It's really astronomical when you think about it. We buy products at pennies on the dollar. We bring it back to our time, sell it and keep ourselves *very strong* in liquid capital. Others, we bring back in gold, invest, in this case in 1922, think of the investment interest gained between then and now! Last week I invested gold in a Swiss bank, with the stipulation that they could use it as loan guarantees against their bank, at a higher interest rate than normal, again in 1922. Do you have any idea how much interest we gained in almost one-hundred years? All of this is through the organization, of course. Here's the kicker. I time traveled back to do this transaction last Monday. I left here at noon and came back at noon. Granted, I did spend six hours at the bank in Zurich. Between compounding interest and the value of gold increasing over almost a century, we now have made over forty million dollars! Plus, we still have the gold in Zurich. The reality was between starting the procedure, obtaining everything, selling it in our time, going back and investing it in Zurich, took about three weeks. Once we had the capital to invest in Zurich, it was off to Zurich for six hours and back in the same moment.

This is the beginning of this particular investment. So we'll sort, sell, buy, and process, then go back and invest."

Mark was again amazed. "How did all of this start? Have any members ever stolen anything?"

Steve smiled "Never any theft ever. As I say, the Organization of Time Travelers, the O.T.T. as we abbreviate it, has never in its history ever had a dishonest act from one of its members. They got the original ball rolling long before our time utilizing bartering. It must be stated it appears that time traveling is a relatively 'new phenomenon.'" In explaining, Steve Craig raised his hands in quotes for the words "new phenomenon."

"From what we gather, time travelers started existing somewhere around the very late 1700's. Again it's one of those mysteries we don't really know too much about, or understand, for that matter. The only instance where I know of an O.T.T. member acting a bit against the grain was a man named Brian Fields."

"Oh yes! Arthur not only told me about Brian Fields but brought me back to the Key West Cemetery and showed me his mausoleum, as well explained his story. He's in a loop," Mark offered.

"Exactly!" Steve said, with his index finger raised. "However, it also must be said that Brian Fields met with the members of the O.T.T. and cleared it, knowing full well the potential consequences. He was okay with it and because of that, so were we. A good guy who really didn't want to be a time traveler and in being one found his niche in a previous time.

Now, as far as the items from your satchel go, I'll begin processing them tomorrow. We'll get you involved in this end of the business so that eventually you can do the complete processing and investing on your own.

Meanwhile, I believe Arthur mentioned that you own your house? It's kind of like that. What we need to do is time travel back to 1934 actually and buy the house. It's on the market actually, for $1,700.00. You'll buy it outright, then you'll need to put it in the company name. In that contract, you'll be the one who is signing for the corporation. I'll get the appropriate paperwork to do so. I'll go with you as your corporate attorney which, by the way, I am.

Once that is completed, we'll time travel back here and set you up with the corporation's paperwork. You'll then go to the real estate office that has been handling the rent for the property. They'll stop the monthly rent for you. They won't be thrilled about it, as they get a commission for every month's rent, but that's the way the cookie crumbles. We're a good client for them, as you might imagine, yours is not the only property they handle for us here. Oh, the rent collected since we started renting it out, is in a special account, which is in the company name, albeit is yours. As you know, it's been renting to you for these past five years at $2,200.00 a month. Over twelve months that $26,400.00 a year and over the five years you've been there is around $132,000.00 or so, depending on when you moved in. Then minus the $150.00 per month real estate commission, which is $9,000.00, so there's $123,000.00 net, Bear in mind, however, that the house has been rented for decades. I haven't looked, but that is going to add up enormously. The amount in that account has to be well into the hundreds of thousands of dollars. It wasn't always renting for $2,200.00, but you get the point. Oh! I didn't think of maintenance, insurance, and improvements, but it will still be very substantial."

Naturally, Mark found all of this flabbergasting.

"When do you want to go?" Mark inquired.

"Let me get into period clothing and look like a 1934 lawyer. I'll also need to gather the correct paperwork for the purchase, not forgetting the required check from the bank back then. Even in 1934, these things are complicated! As you know, we never know why we're chosen to be time travelers. I have a feeling one of the reasons you were chosen is because of all the period clothing you've always worn! On the flip side, we have a period suit ready for you as well," Steve said with a laugh.

There was a closet in his office which he opened. He pulled out a suit hanging in a bag and handed it to Mark. "Tailored to your exact measurements. It should fit perfectly."

Mark recalled the clothes in Paris that were waiting for him. With that already established, he had no cause to doubt or question.

After they were dressed, Mark looked in the mirror. He then looked at Steve.

Laughing, he said, "You look like Herbert Hoover!"

Steve laughed and did a perfect touché. "And you look like a gunsel bodyguard!"

"A gunsel, eh?" He laughed back. It brought to mind the young thug in The Maltese Falcon movie who worked with Sidney Greenstreet.

Bogart referred to him as a gunsel several times in that 1941 film noir.

Mark liked the term, not to mention the suit that went with it.

Steve grabbed an old style brown leather briefcase. It had a flap top with two straps located at the 1/3 points and a central snap lock.

"Everything is in order. Okay, let's go to January 3, 1934, Key West, the corner of Southard and Bahama streets, twelve noon sharp. Now shake my hand!"

They shook hands and once again, things started spinning and a lightheaded feeling came across both of them. The next thing they knew, they were standing on the corner of Southard and Bahama streets.

Suddenly a beautiful Packard Sport Phaeton pulled up.

"Hey Spotty!" Steve called out to the driver.

The automobile was nothing less than magnificent. Mark knew a bit about classic cars and this was indeed one of the finest examples of automobiles of its era. While there may have been an equal, here and there, there certainly wasn't a better automobile on the road. A V12 engine, four door convertible that was capable of over 100 MPH. Magnificent was no exaggeration. Steve was engaged in conversation with the man driving the car. They apparently were well acquainted, judging by the shared laughter. Mark stood off to the side amazed by the sound of twelve cylinders idling.

There was nothing like a twelve cylinder engine. Smoother than any other piston engine in existence. Mark recalled that Enzo Ferrari marveled at the Packard V12 and credited it for his reasoning to build all Ferraris as twelve cylinders. "A Ferrari is a twelve cylinder car," he recalled a quote of Ferrari's.

However, here it was, 1934. At this stage of the game, Enzo Ferrari hadn't built his own first car yet was the racing director for Alfa Romeo. Still, the Packard V12 idled with the smoothness of a sewing machine as Steve and his friend in the car laughed and carried on pleasantries.

After a few minutes, they shook hands and the Packard pulled slowly away.

"That's Morgan Spottsgrave III. They are a very, very old family here in Key West. In our time, they have law offices on Fleming Street that you may have seen. Well, Spotty, as those familiar with him call him, is a lawyer as well. He has handled our real estate transactions in this time period. I let him know that we were making a purchase today and that we'd need his assistance once again. He's very successful, as you might have noticed by his brand new Packard. We could buy three of the houses we're getting today for the price of that Packard, and that's no exaggeration, I assure you!

"We're heading across the street and down just a hop-skip-and a jump to 506 Southard St," Steve stated. "Here's the real estate office we need. Colby's Real Estate. Andy Colby is the man we'll see. Again, we've done business with him before, so he knows me," Steve said, pointing to the building.

Mark knew the building. It had been a craft beer bar in his time, which unfortunately had closed. Here it was, over eighty years younger and a real estate office, not the bar he knew. Not a bar at all.

They crossed the street and entered the office. The door had a mild squeak to it and a spring attached to its middle cross bar which pulled it closed behind them, almost rudely.

"Hello, Andy! How are you?"

"Why it's that good old Steve Craig! How are you, Steve?" Andy got up and shook hands with Steve.

Andy was in his early forties; slim, blond hair, well dressed for the period and had a spring to his step. Clearly, he was someone who enjoyed life and life enjoyed him.

"Well, everything is good and hopefully it will be good for you as well, as we are hoping to purchase one of your properties today! You have a listing on the 700 block of United Street."

"Yes, that's the Taylor property. We just listed it!"

"I know! Excuse me, please let me introduce my associate, Mark Straight," laying a friendly hand on Mark's shoulder. "He's a member of the firm."

"How do you do Mark! Greetings and salutations indeed!" Andy Colby said with a grin.

They shook hands. Andy had a sure hand shake and looked Mark directly in the eye in doing so.

"Likewise to you as well," Mark said with a smile.

Why wouldn't he smile? Here he was shaking hands with a man who was going to sell him the house he's been living in for the last five years, albeit over eighty years in the future and at one point or another, he would also handle the leasing of the property, collecting several hundred thousand dollars on his behalf in doing so. Additionally, the man seemed to have a very good nature about himself.

"Please gentlemen, let's sit in my office," Andy said.

They went in and Andy Colby closed the door, which had a large glass window. A ceiling fan whirled. Andy Colby sat behind the desk. Like Mark and Steve, he also wore a suit. His suit was a dark charcoal with black pinstripes.

"Okay, so you're interested in the Taylor property, you were saying?" Andy Colby inquired cheerfully.

"Yes, we are. I've done some homework on the property Your listing is for $1,700.00," Steve said in a matter of fact sort of way, then adding a slight chuckle.

"Indeed you have done your research, as always Steve!"

"Here's what I'd like to offer. I have a check here issued by The Commerce Bank of Key West for that said amount. What I ask is that they cover the closing costs, which I think is reasonable" Steve stated and laid the check on Andy Colby's desk.

"I will be more than happy to present your offer to Mr.Taylor. Let me give him a call and see if he's home. If you could excuse me for a few minutes gentlemen? Have a seat up front and help yourself to the lemon-aid. It's ice cold!"

Steve and Mark got up and before they were out of Andy Colby's office, Andy was at a phone box on the wall next to his desk winding a crank on the side.

"Hello, Ester! It's Andy Colby. Can you ring Zeke Taylor for me, please... Hello, Zeke! Hey, I have a client who's interested in your house! I've known him for a while and he's bought several properties with me. He's a qualified prospect..."

Steve and Mark sat in a couple of chairs out front and chatted a bit. Steve told Mark that the company at this time owned six properties in Key West and intended on buying more.

"It just makes so much sense. We come back to this time period and buy a house, let's say one of the larger ones, as an example. Hypothetically, we pay twelve thousand for it. Jump back to our time and sell it for $1.3M. For you and me, we're gone for a day or so. The house, however, goes through over eighty years of tenants, maintenance, insurance and income. The last is key because, over the years, our bank account is inflating all of the time via rent and the property has paid itself off. Yes, there are expenses and renovations required, but the reality of that is quite trivial. We actually set up an internal loan to ourselves. The rent collected goes to expenses and paying off the loan. It's set for fifteen years. It's 1934 now, so by this time in 1950, it's paid off, so to speak. We've also tossed in a bit of interest."

"This is all staggering information, I was thinking..."

Suddenly Andy Colby burst through the door full of excitement and grinning.

"Zeke Taylor is good with your offer! I can have the paperwork done within twenty-four hours. How does tomorrow at one in the afternoon sound, here in the office?"

"That sounds good to me Andy!" Steve paused. "Hey, I have one question. Why didn't you ask if we wanted to see the house?"

Andy laughed. "I didn't because you gave me an offer, so I knew you were serious. Besides, you've purchased five properties from me. You know if there was anything wrong with any of them, I'd let you know before you could actually put a deposit down. Only an idiot would not watch out for a valued client."

They all laughed and Steve said, "Look, here's the check. If you would, place it with the paperwork so we can close tomorrow."

"Very good, sir! I will have everything ready at one tomorrow!"

Mark was a bit puzzled by the quickness of it all. "Tomorrow? Does the owner have time to move out that quickly?"

Andy's eyes widened. "Actually, the home is vacant. The owner, Zeke Taylor, is a fisherman and wants to expand from one boat to two. So the house is ready as we speak."

"That's great! So, one pm tomorrow!" Mark replied with enthusiasm.

Andy saw them to the door, he shook both of their hands.

"Steve, again, thank you very much! Mark, a pleasure indeed! We'll see you tomorrow!" Then, with a spring to his step and a light, airy whistle from his lips, headed back into the office.

Steve and Mark exited the building. "Let's grab some lunch! I know a place right around the corner on Duval Street that we can go."

"That sounds splendid! I'm hungry! Oh, look! There's my girlfriend Glades up on the corner! Hey Glades!" he hollered to her.

However, one of the Coke-a-Cola trucks muffled his outcall.

Steve suddenly grabbed his arm. "No! You can't call out to her! She doesn't know you yet. You met her in 1935 and right now it's 1934!"

"Oh shit!" Mark proclaimed.

"Yes, that's one of the things we must be careful and astute about."

Glades and her friend, a girl Mark didn't know, came in their direction on the sidewalk and passed. Mark took note of both of the girls. The other girl was quite attractive as well. She had straight, medium brown hair, was about 5' 4" and maybe about 120 lbs. They were speaking in Spanish and as they passed, Mark gave them both the inquisitive eye, with a smile. They both smiled back.

The men continued to Duval Street and Steve pointed to the La Concha Hotel, off to the right and across the street. "You, of course, know the La Concha, it's been here forever. They have a bar we can grab a bite at."

Right off Duval, in the center of the classic building, was the bar. They went inside, grabbed two stools and Mark marveled at the beautiful display of various ornate liquor bottles on the shelves behind the bar.

"How are you Raulito?" Steve said to the bartender.

"Hello, Steve! Que paso?" Replied the bartender. He was in his late forties, black hair, a large frame, but not heavy.

"Everything is good, Raulito. This is my friend and business associate, Mark. Mark, this is Raulito."

They shook hands and exchanged greetings and Mark greeted him in Spanish. "Mucho gusto!"

Oh! Do you speak Spanish? I'm from Cienfuegos, Cuba originally. I've been here for over twenty years though."

"My Spanish is lacking. It's better than my French, however." Mark replied and a quick flashback to his travels in Paris and talking with Pablo Picasso at Gertrude Stein's salon, crossed his mind in a flash.

"My English isn't too bad, I guess. They wouldn't have me working the bar otherwise," Raulito said with a laugh, then continued "I knew my English had gotten to the point of being beyond mumbo-jumbo when I started dreaming in English!"

Everyone laughed. Raulito was a natural behind the bar. It's a knack one has or doesn't have.

"Raulito, I think today I'll have a midnight sandwich, please."

"Okay, great, one midnight, and you Mark?"

"Wow, a midnight sounds perfect! Not too filling either. Yes please, make it two."

"Gotcha!" Raulito said. He then walked over to a cone shaped mouthpiece at the end of a three-inch wide tube. The tube snaked out of the room and into the abyss of the grand hotel that the bar was located in.

Raulito hollered into the tube, covering the open parts between the opening and his face,

"¡Oye! ¡Necesito dos sandwiches de medianoche!" It wasn't anything that could be construed as being even remotely subtle. Mark's limited Spanish worked fine here. It translated to "Hey! I need two midnight sandwiches!"

A voice came back through the tube "Que?", which means "What?"

Raulito rolled his eyes and breathed a semi-frustrated sigh, then returned to the tube. "Coño!!! Alberto! ¡Necesito dos sandwiches de medianoche!"

The far away voice returned from the tube "Si! Si! Si! Dos medianoches!"

"Si! Gracias!" Raulito replied, breathing a sigh of relief,

The medianoche, or the midnight in English. What a great sandwich! Many see it as most likely the mother of the Cuban sandwich. After all, it has almost all the same ingredients, save for the type of bread used, and it's smaller.

The medianoche was originally from Havana's theater district. People would go out and see a show, and when it was over, head to the cafes in the area for a small bite to eat. The medianoche was ideal. Virtually the same as a Cuban sandwich, however about sixty percent the size, additionally, it also uses medianoche bread, which is a sweet egg bread.

Raul was a very congenial sort. He was also completely mad about automobiles.

He addressed Steve with exuberance, blurting out, "Have you seen that brand new Packard Sport Phaeton V12 that Mr. Spottsgrave just got? It's the talk of the town, I'll tell you. Even people who could care less about cars are talking about it!"

"I saw that car for the first time today. Magnificent is the only way to describe it, I would say."

Suddenly the sandwiches were delivered to the bar. A couple of beers and midnight sandwiches, over talk of Packards, Duesenbergs, Cords, and Pierce-Arrows. Life was good even though this was the Depression, here at the bar at the La Concha hotel, the talk was that of unadulterated opulence.

They finished lunch and bid Raulito a good day, stepping out under the overhang of La Concha.

"Let's go to my house. I have a few things that require attending to. Plus, we have some time to kill anyway between now and the closing tomorrow." Steve said, then pointed to Fleming St. saying "This way!"

As they headed down Fleming Street, Mark inquired "You mentioned you have several properties here?"

"Actually, WE own several properties here. You're one of us, you know!" Steve laughed, then continued. "It's actually a good investment time for us. The reality of all of this is that this time period is the Depression. We can buy at ridiculous prices. However, understand, while the monetary situation is literally pennies on the dollar, most of the people selling are down and out. We're not carpetbaggers, we believe in compassion and many of these people who are selling are families. We have a few plans available. Most do the buyback plan. In the buyback plan, we buy the house and charge an easily manageable monthly mortgage to the seller so they don't have to move. We feel it's important to keep the Conch families in town!

Being time travelers, we also know that WW II is on the distant horizon and that really marks the end of the Depression. They, of course, don't know this, but the plans we have run anywhere from now until 1942 to 1948. It's a good plan for everyone. What we do is take 40% of their monthly rent and file it in an escrow account. At the end of the term, that 40% goes to their credit in buying the house back from us," Steve concluded.

"What? So let's just say that hypothetically speaking their rent is $100 a month. Forty percent of that, or forty dollars, goes into an escrow account that gets credited back to them at the end of their lease? You're kidding, or I'm confused. No one does that!" Mark said. He, like anyone else would be, was astonished at the plan.

"I'm not kidding and you're not confused. It's a good deal for everyone. People stay in their houses and we pretty much break even on the deal. The town stays intact. We also have people that are moving regardless. Or, in your case, the house is being sold in order to purchase a second boat. Some want to leave town. Island living just isn't for them. Those properties we keep, such as yours and mine for instance.

Yours will be like mine in that we buy them in 1934, live in them for a while, maybe rent them out for seventy-five years or so! HA HA! We've done that with a few. Mine actually is always available. You'll see. It's a good size, so if there are more than one of us in town at the same time, there's breathing room for all. It also has a garage, which you'll see is important as well. Oh, we turn here on Elizabeth St. It's just a block over."

They walked up Elizabeth Street. It was the same here in 1934 as it was over eight decades later, in their own time. It was gorgeous. The beauty of what is known as Old Town always amazed Mark and, as it turned out, Steve as well.

"This town, in so many ways, is preserved so well. It actually looks better in our time, than it does right here and here I find it breathtaking!" He commented as they walked up to Elizabeth Street, between Fleming and Southard streets.

"It never gets old, as the saying goes, metaphorically speaking," Mark replied.

192

As they approached Southard Street Steve pointed to the house on the corner across from them.

"Here we are! 600 Elizabeth Street. Home sweet home!"

The first thing that struck Mark was that it had large sapodilla trees in front. The house was clearly a beauty as well, with a wrap around veranda on both levels, ornate wood work railings with lattice all around. One curiosity was as it sat on the corner, it appeared to be on Southard Street, however, the address was on the smaller side of the house, on Elizabeth.

The main entrance was a double, side-by-side door. An interesting curiosity of the house was that this side was virtually entirely fixed, wooden jalousies, no doubt designed to ward off the morning sun. The driveway, directly next to it, was long enough to park a car. The garage was set back several feet and was secured with double side-by-side, barn-style doors. The doors had a row of windows, which took up the top quarter of the door. Above the door, Mark noted a good-luck horseshoe. The windows were dark, however, and you couldn't see in. Mark was curious about the garage, as Steve made note of it. The dark windows only enhanced his curiosity. Above the garage appeared to be a room. There was a window in the second floor of the A-frame structure above the garage door, albeit with closed storm shutters. Though set back from the main facade of the home, the garage was attached.

They entered and Steve let out a sigh of satisfaction. "It's always good to be home, no matter *what* time period it is!" He then let out a laugh. Although Mark really hadn't known Steve all that long, at least in the traditional sense, he felt they were kindred spirits.

"Oh! Before I go any further, I must quell the curiosity I intentionally stirred regarding the garage!" Steve proclaimed as he set his keys on a table as they entered.

"You did a good job of it Steve! I must admit, the dark glass on the garage doors only peaked my interest."

Steve led the way, opening a door to the left, which lead into the garage. He turned on the light, then proclaimed "Here's my baby!"

"Low and behold, the greatest car of it's era, the Duesenberg SJ Dual-Cowl Phaeton!" Steve proclaimed as he flicked the light on.

Mark's jaw dropped. This was perhaps the most magnificent automobile he had ever seen in his life. If he was impressed with Morgan Spottsgrave III's Packard, this left him speechless. It was big. Really big. As a matter of fact, it took up virtually the whole garage, with almost no room to spare. Even in such a confined setting, the car was flat out stunning.

"It's brand new actually. Delivered here two weeks ago. Are you familiar with the Duesenberg J and SJ series at all, Mark?"

"Well, I know a little about Duesenbergs, though not intimately. I do know that they were one of the true American classics," Mark replied.

"Mark, indeed they were! Speaking for myself, the Duesenberg was the finest car of its era. Let me show you something."

Steve then opened the right side cowl engine cover. His enthusiasm for the vehicle was strikingly apparent. It was akin to that of a teenager.

"Look at this engine!"

The light was surprisingly good and the engine and firewall sparkled with reflection. The green engine was massive. Everything was so clean on it, even the intake, which one expected on a car of this era to be a bit greasy. This was so clean you could eat off of it.

"The engine was nothing short of spectacular! It's a straight-eight! When was the last time you saw one of those? 420 cubic inches, or 6.9 liters in metric, look at it! Double overhead cams, in this car! Four valves per cylinder, supercharged. The engine was built for Duesenberg by Lycoming!"

Steve was clearly in his element. He raised his index finger and continued.

"Just for an example, a Mercedes-Benz of the same year, the 500K, one of the most sought after cars in our time, and what a great car it was, also had a straight eight engine and theirs was supercharged as well, produced one-hundred and sixty horsepower. The car could go one-hundred miles an hour. Pretty impressive for 1934, wouldn't you say?"

Steve then laughed loudly and arched backward.

"This Duesenberg has three-hundred and twenty horsepower. We're talking about a car built in 1934, mind you! This car will go over one-hundred and thirty-five miles an hour! Arthur has a boat tail version, with the same engine. That will go even faster! Maybe a touch over one-forty with a tail wind!"

"Oh my God! You're kidding! Will this car go one-hundred and thirty-five miles per-hour? It has three-hundred and twenty horsepower?" Mark was clearly amazed.

"Oh yes! It was so advanced in its day! Here, open the door and have a look inside!"

Mark opened the driver's door as Steve lowered the hood. The door handle clicked like that of a fine jewelry box. As it opened, it was clearly quite heavy, yet swung open easily with refinement, as though it was on ball-bearings.

The smell of opulent leather first hit Mark's olfactory senses before any visual sensations did. Cars of his era didn't come close to rivaling this. The smell of leather permeated his senses as the door swung open with the balance of a bank vault. The first thing that caught Mark's eye was the inside of the door as it opened.

It was no wonder that the fragrance of leather struck him first. The door panel was full leather, armrest included. The top of the door was as expertly crafted woodwork as could be found in the finest cabinetry and furniture in the world.

The woodwork comprised of two different kinds of wood and formed at the top of the door, extending down four inches. Mark guessed it was a cherry with pine, coated with a very substantial amount of varnish. Evenly spaced from one end of the door to the other, no more than an inch tall, inlaid in white Mother-Of-Pearl were a heart, spade, clubs, and heart reproductions from a deck of cards.

As he looked inside, the steering wheel was huge. Behind it, the dash was in aluminum with the gauges offset to the right.

Steve suddenly burst out, "Oh wait! Let me do this right! Let's pull it out of the garage for you to see it properly!"

He then started opening the barn-style garage doors. Steve came back, got in, started the car and pulled out into the driveway and shut it off. The automobile was nothing short of stunning. It was a four door convertible. The rear section also had a small, glass windscreen to deflect the air from the rear passengers when the top was down. The engine cowling was a light beige, while the fenders and rear of the car were a dark navy blue. The windshield was raked about 15 degrees and the convertible top matched the engine cowling in color.

This car was a combination of total state of the art technical achievements of its era, combined with being a rolling piece of art. Additionally, it was huge.

"Let me fill you in a bit on the Duesenbergs. You know, Duesenberg never built a complete automobile?"

"What do you mean?"

"Duesenberg built the chassis. When they were finished with the chassis, they would test drive every single one at the Indianapolis Motor Speedway at over 100 miles-per-hour. The rolling chassis came with everything that made the car go, along with the hood, all the lights, windshield, the dash, and the gauges. But after that, the cars were sent to the buyer's preferred coach builders, who would build the body and interior. Every car was different. This car has a body by LaGrande. Cat out of the box, LaGrande was actually an in house affair they did. However, regardless of what coach builder was used, Duesenberg sold the chassis separately.

Now get this. This car's chassis alone cost $9,500.00! That's about $3,000 more than the Packard V12 of Spottie's we saw earlier! In 1934 terms, $9,500 would pay the annual salary of three doctors! And we *still* don't have a body on it! Now after we put the LaGrande body on the car, the way we wanted it, total cost was $19,935.00!

198

Now, in our time, that would be around $365,000.00. We could buy eleven of your houses with it! However, this is a long term investment. We buy it for the price of a Honda Civic in our time, take good care of it over the years, then we sell it in our time for between $9 and $11 million. It's a great investment! We'll most likely list it with Sotheby's in a few months, uh, that would be a few months in our regular time. Ha Ha!"

"Holy shit!"

Steve then continued "I will say that we put twenty percent of the net profits to charities. It's on a graduating scale for everything we do. We are firm believers in helping our fellow man. Some are charities, while other times it might just be anonymously making a donation to someone who is good, but in need. They never know it's us either." He started laughing. "There was one guy, a good man, but he really doesn't care for me all that much. He'll never know that I'm the one who saved his ass!"

They both laughed and Mark shook his head.

Mark peered into the interior and saw the gauges. They were mounted in a brush-aluminum finish with the ornate wood on the top of the dash. Everything made sense, there was a clock, a speedometer with odometer, temperature gauge, oil pressure gauge, and another which said "Alt".

"Steve! What's this? An altimeter?"

"Ha Ha! Yes! They come with an altimeter! You know what? Let's take her for a ride! Hop in the other side!"

Mark needed no prodding for this. He ran around to the other side, opened the heavy, ball bearing bank vault door and hopped in.

Steve then said "Oh! Look at the odometer! Only 124 miles! Welcome to my Deusy!" He exclaimed, reaching out to shake Mark's hand. When he did, suddenly Mark realized Steve was pulling some sort of time traveling prank on him. Everything started swirling again, albeit very quickly returned and they were right where they started, in Steve's driveway in the Duesenberg.

"What happened? It felt like a time travel, but we never went anywhere," Mark asked, shaking his head for a bit.

"Ha Ha! Look at the odometer!"

Mark looked over at the odometer. It now read 3,297! His jaw dropped.

"You see, in 1934 the hurricane of 1935 hadn't happened yet! We went five years into the future. The Overseas Highway has been completed for about a year now, and it's much better than a ride around town! Plus, maybe we can catch dinner up the Keys and kill two birds with one stone!"

Mark laughed and shook his head. Time traveling for the sake of a nicer drive. This was ridiculous, albeit ridiculous in a great way.

Steve started the Duesenberg's straight eight. It sounded 85% like a V8 and 15% like an inline six. The supercharger had a whine to it.

"At low RPM, the supercharger draws thirty-five horsepower," Steve said as he engaged the clutch, put it in gear, and left the driveway.

Mark was amazed at how much Steve knew about the car. It was a true passion for him and he beamed while driving the massive machine.

When they got to Bayview Park, Mark realized he hadn't been out here since he started time traveling back to old Key West. There was water everywhere! The road continued, however, it was all surrounded by marshland and water! New Town didn't exist yet! Now he recalled that day he was out on Glades deck looking at the beautiful view of Fish Bone Lane and commenting on how beautiful Old Town looked. Glades was confused by the term. Here lay the explanation! New Town didn't exist yet!

Once they cleared Key West the road continued without incident. There was virtually no traffic to deal with. The bridges were, however, the old bridges. These bridges were built on the former train bed and bridges. They were very narrow.

As they crossed one Steve pointed out, "These bridges are so slim that often trucks passing each other in opposite directions lose their mirrors to each other. This being such a big automobile, I need to stay alert for this!"

Once they cleared Stock Island things started to look familiar. Funny, not much changed here in over eighty years. Boca Chica Channel looked exactly the same, with the exception that the lower side was fully absent of liveaboards.

When they got to the bridge linking East Rockland Key with Boca Chica, Steve gunned it. The engine roared, the wind was howling as they accelerated up to about seventy-five miles per hour.

"I'm still in second gear and we're at seventy-five miles per hour. They say this car will go over one-hundred in second gear! Remarkable!" Then laughing said, "Of course it only has three-speed transmission!" He then paused before continuing, "It's a non-synchro transmission. HA HA! Right about now over in Germany Dr. Porsche is designing V16 racing cars for a company called Auto-Union, later known as Audi. He hadn't invented the synchronized transmission yet!"

When they arrived at Boca Chica Steve backed off down to around thirty-five miles per hour. In this area, the road just wasn't designed for faster travel in this day and age. It wasn't like the road of today. It was a combination of coral rock, limestone, and sea shells pressed down together with a steamroller. Tarmac for the Overseas Highway in this section was still in the future. The best places to drive in many areas were the bridges.

From above was the distinctive sound of a radial engine airplane. Several in fact! They were Navy fighters and trainer bi-planes flying out of the Boca Chica air station. They were returning after exercises and seemed to be just lumbering in. It was still a rush to see, however.

Steve pulled the Duesenberg over, shut off the engine, and engaged the handbrake. "Let's look at these planes fly in for a bit!"

"Great idea! Stopping to smell the roses, so to speak!" Mark agreed.

They got out and stood on the roadside watching the planes return to the airbase.

The very first one came in with obvious engine trouble. The engine was smoking a bit and had a clear misfire. Although they were quite a ways from the landing strip, it was clear that it landed safely as the remainder of the exercise continued to land. If there was trouble on the ground the others would be diverted to another runway, which they were not. Some came in smooth and quickly, other slow and wobbly.

Mark spoke out saying "Once these planes are within range, they can just glide in! Quite a contrast to an F/A 18 or an F35. If their engine goes, they're a virtual brick!"

Steve laughed a chuckle and nodded. Mark, in the meantime, pulled out his iPhone and snapped pictures of the planes coming in. He also filmed the last few flying into the airfield. After all the planes were in, everything was very, very quiet. Additionally, the air was still. Just the sound of standing on the rough road seemed loud.

Steve smiled and motioned for them to continue the journey north, destination unknown. They got back into the Duesenberg with the doors giving a very secure sound when closing.

Mark instinctively looked for a seat belt. He had also done this back at Steve's house as well, only realizing that this was 1934 and seat belts didn't exist yet. Steve disrupted the tranquility of the moment when he started the big 420 cid/6.9L straight-eight cylinder engine, Suddenly a flock of egrets took to flight out of the marsh on the other side of the road, startled no doubt, by the non-organic rumble. Steve put it into gear and eased out the clutch. He pulled back onto Overseas Highway with a lot of care for the machine itself.

The drive up the Keys was enlightening, no doubt about that. So much was not developed at this time. At Mile Marker 20 Mark observed a small, quaint former train stop. He knew this in his time as a restaurant/bar named Mangrove Mama's. The train stop still had the water tower to service the steam locomotives that had passed through between 1912 and 1935. The tower looked familiar. Was this the same water tower that was at Blue Heaven restaurant in Key West in his regular time?

Steve continued up the Keys, meandering across the islands, key after key, in a lazy fashion. Suddenly he proclaimed, "This is what we've been waiting for!"

There, clearly to be seen ahead around a right-hand corner in all of its grand majesty, was the Bahia Honda Bridge.

The Bahia Honda Bridge was not like any of the other bridges in the Keys, which were low bridges built on the former Overseas Railroad bed. The Bahia Honda Bridge was just under a mile long and built as steel truss bridge with a superstructure, because the channel it traverses is by far, the deepest channel in the Keys (Bahia Honda means Deep Channel in Spanish). With the superstructure being too narrow for a two lane highway to be built on the former railroad bed, they built the highway *on top* of the superstructure! Majestic is nothing short of accurate and here, in 1934, she was in her absolute prime!

"Let's give the girl some exercise!" Steve hollered as he gunned the car on the approach to the bridge on Spanish Harbor Key. When he got to the bridge, he up shifted into high gear.

"70 miles per hour!" Steve shouted excitedly as he raced up the rise, the Duesenberg projectile flying up the road built on top of the bridge's superstructure. The straight-eight roared and the car continued accelerating. At the top of the rise at the entrance of the bridge, where it leveled out, Steve hollered again "Ninety-five!"

The road was beautiful and there was not another vehicle in sight. The engine continued to propel the car yet faster as the wind howled.

"115!"

The bridge rose with a bubble rise about mid-way. Heading on the down slope Steve hollered out "130!"

Mark interjected at this point "Hey Steve! If we get killed in 1934 how does it affect us?"

"We go into a loop! Arthur told you about Brian Fields perhaps? 133!"

He let off the throttle and the car started to slow down. As the Duesenberg was the aerodynamic equivalent to that of a house, it slowed quickly.

"These Duesys can go like the wind, but suspension technology isn't all that more advanced from a Conestoga wagon! The brakes are like the Conestoga as well!"

When they got to the end of the bridge they were going about fifty miles per hour. To be frank and to the point, Mark was quite relieved. While it was a truly amazing experience, he was glad it was over. Doing over one-hundred and thirty miles an hour over the

Bahia Honda Bridge was a tale he knew his friend Blackheart would relish almost as much as the jukebox.

"You know, regarding the loop, we think one might be able to change history on the next loop or two, so long as it only affects ourselves and no one else. We're not sure though, as this has never happened, so far as we know." Steve continued as they continued north on US1 at a civilized speed.

"I'm glad we are not the first to try it out," Mark said, with a sigh of relief. Steve laughed.

They continued up the Keys, crossing the Seven Mile Bridge to Marathon. In Marathon, Steve pulled over at a roadside restaurant where they had dinner. It wasn't a fancy establishment at all, but the dinner was reasonable. Fish, as one might expect, was the order of the day. Steve had grouper while Mark had the dolphin. It was a Cuban owned restaurant, which Mark got a kick that on the menu, as they listed the fish in Spanish, mero and dorado. They had the flavors of Cuba in them as well. It was a good dinner, by all means. They offered beer as well, Budweiser and Schlitz. Mark had the Schlitz and noted it had more body than the commercial beers of his time.

When they headed back it was dark. Crossing the Seven-Mile Bridge was beautiful, with the nearly full moon glistening on the water. It, however, couldn't compare with the Bahia Honda Bridge. When they had been going north it was breathtaking as the Duesenberg roared across it at over one-hundred and thirty miles an hour, scaring the wits out of Mark and inspiring a bit of an adrenaline rush for Steve.

This ride was at a leisurely forty miles an hour. Compared to the ride up, Mark felt he could get out and walk next to the car. However, with a relaxed, easy drive, the view was incredible. Here they were, over sixty feet above the moonlit water, on a crystal-clear evening. They could see for miles and miles. The Gulf of Mexico glimmered in the moonlight off to their right, while the Atlantic Ocean did likewise off to their left. They rode the dividing line. Way out in the distance, several miles, they could see Sombrero Light's warning illumination from its Fresnel lens. It was built in an eighteen-fifties way out on a former island, originally known as Sombrero Key. Like many islands in the Keys, they come and go. Sombrero Key washed away and became a reef. As they motored on, both looking at the light, Mark made the observation "You know, in this time, right now as we speak, there is a crew out there manning that lighthouse. Imagine being out there right now! That's just incredible!"

Steve agreed "You can say that again!"

They eventually got back to Steve's house in Key West. Mark got out and opened the garage doors, while Steve backed the Duesenberg in. Mark closed the doors. Steve got out and reached to shake Mark's hand saying, "We have to go back to 1934! Don't forget, we jumped a few years for the sake of the drive!"

Mark laughed and shook Steve's hand and they both fell into the time travel, emerging seconds later, exactly where they were, albeit in 1934.

Steve had Mark stay in the bedroom on the west side of the house. There were five bedrooms in the house and Steve's master bedroom was on the east side. It was a comfortable room, with nightstands on either side of the bed and a full desk on the other side of the room.

Before he turned in for the evening he sat at the desk and looked at the photographs in his iPhone he had taken earlier, while in the car and in Marathon. In the small screen, they all looked good. He knew it would look much better in his computer when he got home tomorrow, over eighty years in the future. Fortunately, the electricity was the same in 1934 as it was in his own time, nine decades in advance. He plugged it in and recharged it overnight.

The next day Mark was up early at 7:15. Heading downstairs he was greeted with the smell of freshly brewed coffee. Steve was in the kitchen reading The Key West Citizen in his pajamas, slippers, and bathrobe. The last time Mark had seen someone in a bathrobe was when that Englishman walked into the bar in Key West, in what Mark mentally called "Real Time."

"Good morning, Mark! Grab a cup of coffee right there!" He stated, pointing at the percolator, with a cup sitting in waiting. Then he continued joking in a sarcastic tone, "The percolator! It's the latest invention! We're state-of-the-art! Hummmm... has that phrase been invented yet?" He was grinning ear to ear.

Mark sauntered over to the pot, chuckling and poured a cup. Black.

"You know? I only drink it black and it must be poured at a forty-five-degree angle," Mark stated with a wink.

"Forty-Five-degree angle, of course! It's the only way! Besides, we don't have any cream, so you don't have a choice!" Steve proclaimed with a laugh.

It was a beautiful day, blue skies, white puffy clouds, and a light breeze. Mark and Steve enjoyed it, taking it all in.

Mark took a small, cautious sip of his piping hot coffee, took a breath, let out a sigh of satisfaction, then stated, "I'm still coming to terms with all of this time traveling Steve. It's like an extended dream or something? Yet, it's reality. I've spent time in Paris in the 1920's. I have a girlfriend in 1935 Key West. Here we are in 1934 and if I go over to her apartment right now, she'll have no idea who I am. I saw a brand new jukebox here in Key West, again in 1935, and I ended up buying it as an antique in our regular time. I met Pablo Picasso, Gertrude Stein, and F. Scott Fitzgerald. I've actually mixed a drink for the patron saint of alcoholic libations, Ernest Hemingway! I met one guy, then went into a time travel and saw his grave. I just drove one way over the old Bahia Honda Bridge, a structure that I've only seen as a derelict bridge in my own time, a structure that is falling apart into the sea bit by bit, at one-hundred and thirty-three miles an hour one way, then a little over an hour later at a leisurely drive with a full moon lighting the surrounding waters. Today, we're buying a house, the house that I've lived for five years and paid rent in for five years, albeit eighty something years in the future. I'd have to say that the word "surrealistic" is an understatement if there ever was one. So, even though I'm learning the ropes of it all somewhat quickly, I'm still not entirely used to it and find it very odd to deal with."

Steve smiled and joked, "Well, Mrs. Lincoln, other than that unfortunate one-way exchange with your husband and Mr. Booth, how did you like the play?"

They both laughed wholeheartedly and raised their coffee cups in a toast to each other.

A while later they walked down to the real estate office, which was only two blocks from Steve's house. Morgan Spottsgrave was already there, as naturally was Andy Colby. The owner of the property, Zeke Taylor, arrived shortly thereafter.

It was a simple transaction. Much less complicated than that of Mark and Steve's normal time. Six papers to sign, a bank check issued, a title application, utility bills paid off, and they were done. Twenty minutes later they all wished each other well and were on their separate ways.

After they got back to Steve's house, Mark said "Unless we have something to do, I think I'll jump ahead a year and a few months and check on my girl Glades. After that, I'll jump to the office on Stock Island and pick up my things and check out my "new" house! HA HA!"

Steve laughed as well and they bid each other good fortunes. With that, Mark disappeared.

Mark materialized in his home on United Street only a year after he left Steve at his house on Francis Street. It was ten in the morning when he arrived and he felt he could use a pick-me-up, so the first thing he did was hop on his bike and head over to Jack's for a con leche and something to eat for breakfast. He first checked his money to make sure he didn't have any money issued in the future of 1935. All was good there. It carried a large amount of weight when Arthur had told him that when he first experienced time travel. He recalled Arthur telling him all about time travel and what he was in for and how to prepare for it. That was on the beach, just outside of Jack's. It seemed like years since he'd been there, he thought. As a matter of fact, it had been years, so to speak. Since he was here last, he'd been jumping all over both time and the globe!

He was at Jack's in less than two minutes. He parked his bike against a palm tree on the beach and went inside. There was Cynthia and Ol' Beans again. He felt right at home. He sat at the breakfast bar and Cynthia came up to him, greeting him with a smile and even remembered his name.

"Well look what the cat dragged in! How have you been Mark?"

"All's been well, thanks, Cynthia! And you?"

"Aside from being stuck with Ol' Beans six days a week, I can't complain. I have a job and in these times that's a Godsend!"

Suddenly Ol Beans piped in "Oh! Would you listen to her!" Then mimicking her in a high female voice continued "Aside from being stuck with Ol Beans six days a week" then returning to his regular

voice "To the moon, young lady, to the moon! HA HA HA!"
Everyone laughed.

As always, Mark marveled at Ol' Beans cooking apron. It was a complete mess. There would be no way in hell any cook could get away with being such a mess in the twenty-first century. However, that was later, this was now and now was 1935.

"What will you have for breakfast" Cynthia inquired.

"Let's see, I feel like I've been traveling in light years lately. I'd like a con leche, Cuban toast, ham, and eggs, sunny side, with hash browns please."

Cynthia was writing on her order pad and mumbling the order as he gave it to her.

"Hash browns, ham, and eggs sunny, Cuban toast, con leche... okay, got it. One question for ya, what's a light year? Oh wait, no, I really don't have time for the explanation." Then turning to the cook, "Hey Ol' Beans, two eggs sunny, ham, Cuban toast, and browns. I got the con leche!"

He looked behind his seat at the bar and saw what would be his jukebox, or rather in this time period, coin-operated phonograph, that he'd buy many decades later. He was amazed, as always.

Mark was sitting directly across from that brass marvel, adorned with the eagle atop which made the Cuban coffee. As Cynthia started setting up the brew, she turned to Mark.

"Oh, your friend Arthur was here earlier this morning! You only missed him by about a half-hour, I'd say."

"Oh! I didn't know he was in town. I'll have to check in with him!" He replied.

"Yeah! He was here with his family. They were sitting at number 3. We number our tables for the orders. That's the booth right by the door."

"Family?" What the hell, Mark thought.

"Yeah, you know, his wife and baby."

Mark was completely aghast, yet he knew he had to be on his game and not miss a beat.

"Oh, yeah, I just was surprised that he's in town and going out with them."

"It is the cutest baby boy, isn't he? Arthur Jr. He didn't cry once either. Just laughed the entire visit! They said he's six months already!"

"Six months? Time flies."

Cynthia gave him his con leche and headed out to one of her tables. "Thanks!"

Now that she was gone, Mark started absorbing all of this and this was something so surrealistic he had to swallow a sip of coffee prior to pondering.

Arthur, his mentor in time traveling, who was from his time in the twenty-first century, has a wife and baby in 1935. "What the hell???" He thought.

This was something that he pondered throughout breakfast. He left Jack's completely in a light state of shock. Riding over to see Glades was now a second priority, although he was going through the motions. Funny, he thought, he didn't know where Arthur hung his hat in 1935 Key West or in twenty-first century Key West. What he did know was that wherever it was, it was the same place in either century.

He stopped by Steve's house on his way to see Glades. Maybe Steve could shed some light on all of this. However, there was no answer at Steve's house. He must be away, most likely over eighty years in the future.

When he got to Glades apartment over the store on Caroline Street and Bone Fish Lane, she greeted him with a smile and invited him in. They quickly embraced and in seconds were naked and making love. This lasted an hour and a half.

They spent the rest of the day on the waterfront. Oysters on the half shell and turtle soup at the Raw Bar washed down with a couple of ice cold Royals. Glades was working that night at the Victoria. Mark had resigned, no longer needing the job. He was now financially secure and was in and out of 1935. At this point, he was curious how he got the job in the first place. For that matter, he was curious how he landed in Key West. After all, when he first traveled here, he was established in town, with a place to live and a job. All of that would be a quest for another day, however.

After Glades went to work, Mark headed to Sloppy Joe's for a beer. Skinner was at the bar and greeted him with a smile, Skinner had a jet black complexion, which was a complete contrast to his pearl white teeth. The contrast only made his grin more prominent. On the one hand, you couldn't help but like the guy. On the other hand, at over three-hundred pounds and armed with a baseball bat hidden behind the bar, one had to be glad he was on your side.

It was late afternoon and by his second Royal suddenly Ernest Hemingway barreled in and slapped him on the back. "Hey Mark! How are you? What have you been up to?"

Here he was in 1935 Key West and in a short time he'd become a back slapping, drinking, and fishing buddy with Ernest Hemingway.

Ernest continued. "You know? Josie and I are heading to Havana on Pilar tomorrow. We'd be honored if you'd like to join us. We're going to be trawling all the way there. We've been talking and we both like your disposition and outlook. Quite honestly, we can use a hand as well. It's one thing to go out with someone on an afternoon with their wives and girlfriends to have a little picnic on the boat. It's a whole different kettle of fish when you're off for say, a week, with a complement of men, who are all fishing, drinking, and carousing in the bars of Havana. We think you'd fit in well with our stew. What do you say?"

"Holy shit! Yes, It's my honor! Thank you very much, Ernest! How long do you think we'll be gone for?"

"We play these things by ear. There's no set time on them. Having stated that, I'm in the middle of writing a new book. I'm in a bit of a lull right now, so a few days away will do my brain good. It's a day to get there and a day to return. Staying one night in Havana is a gross injustice. Figure at least three nights in Havana. So, all in all, somewhere between five and seven days. There's one catch, however."

"What's that?"

"Under no circumstances suggest we leave. Josie and I do these trips via seat of the pants. We know when it's time to go when it's time. We don't know when that is until it happens. It's an instinct. We had one deck hand with us once who wanted to go back before we even arrived in Havana. I was going to throw his ass overboard!"

"Go back, I'm ready when you're ready. I might need a bit of help with Spanish, I'm a little rusty and limited with that."

"No problem there. I speak fluent Spanish. Josie does too. So time isn't an issue for you?"

"Ernest, I'm a time traveler. Time is never an issue for me."

"Time traveler? What the fuck is a time traveler?"

Mark laughed, "I'll fill you in later on that, but no, time is not an issue for me. Where do we meet and what time?"

"Mole Pier at 9 am tomorrow morning."

"9 at the Mole. Done."

"I'll leave your name at the guard gate, so you'll have clearance at the base."

"I'll be there. What should I bring?"

"How about sandwiches and fruit for the sail over? We can cook our catch on the boat for an early dinner before we roll into Havana. If we don't catch anything, we'll eat there."

"Sounds like a plan!"

Ernest looked up at Skinner and said, "A couple of Royals please, Skinner!"

They came right out of the ice and were perfect temperature, contrasting for the hot day.

Mark and Ernest then toasted their upcoming voyage.

Mark headed to Fausto's Food Palace on Fleming. It was the same market he knew from his time, albeit a different setup inside. Fausto's has a long history. He picked up everything he'd need for the lunch on the boat; ham, cheese, mustard, bread, lettuce. He was good to go.

The next morning he made sandwiches and put them in a lunch box. He wrapped them in wax paper as plastic hadn't been invented yet, much less sandwich bags. There was a small suitcase that he packed as well. A change of clothes would be welcome by the time they arrived in Havana, especially as fishing was involved.

A taxi arrived which took him to the gate of the naval base on Southard Street. The sentry there checked his list and cleared him to enter. It was a bustling area, quite the contrast to the area in his time.

Mark walked down to the dock and found Ernest and Josie already on the boat preparing for the trip.

Ernest piped out loudly when he saw Mark approaching "You're early! We were hoping to have everything done by the time you arrived."

"While I'm not always on time for everything, a trip to Cuba aboard Pilar with Hemingway and Russell is one I'll be early for! Hell, you two would most likely leave my ass in Key West if I was late!"

Everyone laughed loudly.

Mark continued "Request permission to come aboard, Captain!"

"Request approved! Come aboard!"

It was a beautiful day and the water beyond the far pier was calm. It was about 80 degrees and sunny. A perfect day, if there ever was one for heading to Cuba. While Hemingway was checking the engines, Russell was setting the bait on hooks for the trawl over.

Mark stored his things below. Most of the front was some sort of boxes covered in tarps. He found space nonetheless.

Pilar was a fine craft if there ever was one of its era. Mark admired the woodwork she was constructed with. In the twenty-first century, and several decades prior to that, everything was made of fiberglass. He was living in a bygone era, however. This was 1935.

There was a cooler that he opened to store the sandwiches. It had room in it, but only barely. The cooler was filled with Royal crown top cans, a gallon glass jug of water, and a gallon glass jug of orange juice. Pilar was loaded with provisions for the trip.

He heard Ernest fire up the Chrysler and the boat started to vibrate slightly as he put the last sandwiches into the cooler. He came up from below and Ernest said to him "I think we're almost ready to shove off. Let's let the engine warm up a bit, then if you'll get the bow line, Josie will get the stern."

Mark nodded and headed to the front of the boat. For a couple of minutes, Ernest and Josie were talking back and forth. Mark couldn't hear them over the idling six-cylinder marine Chrysler. They weren't talking loud and the engine garbled all that was said.

It really didn't matter, however. After a few minutes, Ernest hollered to Mark, "Okay! Release the line!"

Mark released it and Ernest backed out slowly, then when clear of the docking posts, switched it into forward and turned the vessel around. They motored slowly out of the Mole inlet harbor. There were a few naval ships docked at the Outer Mole. Mark returned to the cockpit where Hemingway and Russell were.

"A couple of tin cans here today." Ernest pointed to a couple of destroyers docked, using their naval nicknames.

They headed out into the aqua-green waters off Key West. Ernest opened her up to about 3/4 throttle and the bow lifted and the stern dug in. After about ten minutes the water became deep, deep navy blue. The break of the water at the bow was so white it seemed to illuminate. This meant that they were in deep water, off the Continental Shelf. Ernest slowed down as Josie prepared to set out the trawling lines he had prepared at the dock. Ballyhoo was the bait of the day.

The Chrysler was shut down and a separate, smaller Lycoming four cylinder was fired up for the trawl and three lines were set out. Amazing. Here was a craft with an engine set out specifically for trawling.

Mark again thought to himself, "This is absurd! Here I am, it's 1935 and I'm aboard Pilar in the Atlantic Ocean, Florida Straits, trawling our way to Havana with Ernest Hemingway and Josie Russell."

Suddenly the port side line started spinning! In the distance behind the craft, perhaps one-hundred yards, a fish leapt from the water, wiggling in an attempt to free itself from the hook that was embedded in its jaw.

"It's a good size wahoo you got there Josie! Reel that bastard in!" Hemingway barked loudly, full of excitement.

Josie Russell was an expert fisherman. It was said that it was he who introduced Hemingway to saltwater sport fishing and that was true. Hemingway had grown up in the midwest freshwater fishing. This big game saltwater fishing was a whole different experience. Josie had introduced Hemingway to it alright however, by 1935, Hemingway had been at it for six years and was long ago an expert himself.

"Come on Josie, you have him!!!" Hemingway roared and shut the engine off.

Suddenly, without warning, the starboard line started spinning! The terrorized fish jumped about four feet out of the water eighty to one-hundred yards behind Pilar.

"Crap! Another Fucking wahoo!" Mark hollered.

In the madness, the center line buzzed and Hemingway grabbed it "We hit a goddamned school of bloody wahoo! Do you know how rare it is to find a school of wahoo?"

The Wahoo. A Pelagic fish, capable of traveling at sixty miles per hour. Many consider it the best-tasting fish in the sea. Three lines out and three lines hooked.

"Spread out! We can't get the lines crossed! Mark, go off to the starboard side of the boat, I'll lean to port side! Ernest you've got the center. Let's cross our fingers and do our best to keep them from crossing. However, these fish are panicking, plus they are way out there, so who knows? We'll just hope for the best!" Josie hollered.

Each angler was doing their best to reel in their fish, trying to steer it clear of the other lines. Panic and mayhem may have been the order of the day, at this point. Before it was a leisurely cruise in the Florida Straits. Now, with the wahoo hooked and all the excitement at hand, pandemonium was also the order of business on board Pilar. Every curse word in the book was erupting from the mouths of each angler. Not that it would offend anyone, at this point, as there was no land in sight and no one to hear them.

Hemingway, the sportsman's sportsman, was going at it like there was no tomorrow with his rod and reel. Here it was, 1935 and Hemingway was thirty-five, full of gusto and a lust for fishing. Mark looked over for an instance and saw the younger man living his passion to the utmost.

That, however, was only for an instant of a second. Mark was far too busy to be distracted longer than that.

"Ernest! Move a bit closer to starboard! Our fucking fish are too damn close! We can't allow their lines to tangle! If they do, we're fucked!" Josie hollered.

"You have that right! Mark! How are you doing?" Ernest cried out, not quite looking at him over his shoulder, but sensing he wasn't too far away by instinct alone.

"As well as can be expected under the circumstances, Captain! I still have the wahoo on the line and I'm reeling the bitch in bit by bit!"

Here they were in the Florida Straits, the sun beat down and sweat was pouring off of all three men. Regardless, they all continued fighting and reeling the fish in.

After over an hour, Mark's was the first to get to the boat.

"Mine is at the boat!" The fish was not happy, flipping in the water's surface, splashing water everywhere.

"Mark! There's a gaffe on the lower side of the stern! You're on your own as we all each have a fish hooked! Good luck!" Josie roared across the boat.

In an instant, Mark stuck his pole into the rod holder on the side of the boat. The gaff was right in front of Ernest. Somehow, in grabbing it, he managed to stay clear of him, returning to his side of the boat with the gaff.

"You have conviction, dexterity, and passion, Mark," Hemingway said, never taking his eyes off of his own fishing line.

At this point, Mark gaffed the fish and struggled to get it over the side of the boat and into the cockpit. It was a big wahoo, well over one hundred pounds. In spite of the fish wiggling left and right, Mark dragged it into the boat like a seasoned deckhand. In doing so, he guided its entry to the center of the cockpit of the boat, away from the two other active, struggling anglers.

"Mine's here! We need to gaff it!" Josie screamed in excitement.

As Mark's fish flipped around on the deck, away from everyone, he once again was gaffing a fish and expertly tossing it to the rear. It was another large one, at least as large as his.

It seemed, as quickly as the fish were originally hooked, they were just as quickly hauled into the boat. Once he had Josie's in the cockpit, Ernest's was ready! Again, with the finesse of a very experienced angler, Mark gaffed the fish and hurled it aboard.

The three men, out of breath, watched the three wahoo slow their panic down more and more as they died.

"Mark, you're a man of prowess and conviction. We're proud you're with us on this excursion. There will surely be more. We're cut from the same cloth." Ernest said, catching his breath. "The fish are noble fish. Each put up an honorable and just fight. I respect these fish. I give them more respect than I do many men."

They steered clear of the fish for five minutes. No one needed a Wahoo's teeth in their foot, ankle, or calf. With the engines off, Pilar was just drifting in calm seas, floating with the Gulf Stream in The Straits of Florida. Meanwhile, the three men sat on the stern of the boat.

There wasn't much chatter. All three knew that what had just happened would never happen again in their lifetimes.

Once the fish had expired, Ernest proclaimed "If there ever was a time for a victory celebration, that would be at this hour. Josie, go below and bring up three ice cold Key West Royal Lagers. They are on the ice in the cooler."

Josie came up with the beers and they opened them and toasted their good fortune. "We must also toast these three wahoo. They each put up a gallant fight and are truly a very noble fish." Mark knew that it would be another two years before Hemingway would go to Spain to cover the civil war there for Alliance Magazine. But the respect he had for the fight the fish gave, and because of the fight, the fish itself, Mark could easily see how Ernest Hemingway would fall in love with Spain. After all, the respect for the fight and the animal was exactly the same with bull fighting.

They all cheered and touched vessels, took long pulls on their beer cans, each one of them downing at least three-quarters of their beverages. They certainly had a thirst. One more quick swig and they were empty. Josie went below for more beer for all. Ernest restarted the Chrysler and they continued their voyage to Havana.

"There's no point in laying the lines out. The sea has been good to us. We shouldn't be greedy," Ernest said to Mark. There was a long pause, perhaps twenty-five seconds as they looked forward to the open waters ahead of them. Then Ernest asked, "So tell us, where did you learn to gaff like that, Mark? That was not the work of an amateur angler. You have experience, and professional at that."

Mark chuckled and looked at Ernest, then Josie. He then took a good size swig on his beer.

"I worked swordfishing boats in Provincetown and Brooklyn." He smiled. "Out of Brooklyn, The Agatha Leigh, and out of Provincetown two boats, the Lady Doris and the Lilly M. Three summers total. I was seventeen on the Lady Doris for a year, then I went down to Brooklyn for a bit and was aboard the Agatha Leigh. I was eighteen at that point. I returned to Provincetown the next summer and worked my favorite boat, the Lilly M."

"You used that gaff like you used it yesterday!" Josie marveled.

"I'm thirty-nine, so we're talking twenty years ago. It felt like yesterday. You don't forget it. It's like riding a bike."

Mark and Josie hung the wahoo from the ceiling of the cockpit.

Ernest spoke from the helm as they cleaned and prepared the fish. "We'll get a good dollar for that wahoo in Havana. Plus, they'll make us dinner with it at Marina Pepe's Bodega. It's right in the harbor in Havana. They marinate it in a special mojo called mojo de ajo. It has twice as much garlic in it than regular mojo! You'll like it. Take my word on it. We'll have a few beers while it marinates at Marina Pepe's. That takes twenty minutes to a half hour, then they cook it on a wood fired grill with palm leaves and serve it with black beans, rice, yuca, and Cuban avocado salad. You'll think you died and went to heaven!"

"He's not lying, Mark! Marina Pepe's Bodega is some of the best food you'll find in Havana, but they cater to the boat and ship crews, plus the dock hands. The working men. Legend has it that last year, four or five guys in suits and ties came there because they heard it was excellent cuisine. Pulled up in a brand new Cord convertible. They went inside and started talking to a dock crane operator and his crew. Apparently, someone said the wrong thing and the four or five of them were swimming in the harbor, suits and all!"

They all laughed loudly, needless to say.

It was about 4:30 when Ernest hollered out "Land Ho! Castillo de los Tres Reyes del Morro, starboard fifteen degrees!"

Mark looked out and ahead, maybe seven miles distant, was the castle entrance to Havana Harbor.

Ernest guided Pilar into Havana Harbor with respect. It was a slow entrance to a respected harbor, as it should be. Mark marveled at the castle which guarded the entrance of the harbor. He knew from history that it dated from the mid 1500's.

Hemingway then spoke freely about the harbor they were entering. "This is the entrance, however, it leads to three separate harbors. They are fine harbors at that. The portion of the name Tres Reyes translates to Three Kings. The castle has been there since 1855."

The castle always impressed all who saw it.

"It never gets old or routine, does it, Ernest?" Josie commented.

"Majestic things never become routine. Should they do, the beholder for which the routine falls has lost the passion of life. It all goes back to Samuel Johnson in 1777. I'm not sure you would know it Josie, would you?" Hemingway asked.

"No, I'm afraid you have me on that Ernest," Josie replied.

"What about you Mark? Are you familiar with it, by chance?"

"Yes, as a matter of fact, I believe I may be. 'When a man is tired of London, he is tired of life.' I studied English literature and prose. Regretfully, Mr. Hemingway, they had none of your works when I went to college," recalled Mark.

"Bah! You're certainly right on target with Samuel Johnson, however," Hemingway burst out, then continued with another inquiry at a more subtle, inquisitive volume. A volume that had a sincere interest in its tone. "Studied English literature and prose? Where?"

"As a Connecticut Yankee, I first thought of attending Yale, naturally. However, after much thought, study and investigation on the matter, I found Fordham University in New York to have a curriculum more suited to my needs and interests."

This coming from a deckhand who only a few hours earlier gaffed, hoisted, and hurled three one-hundred pound plus wahoo into the cockpit of Pilar.

Ernest raised an eyebrow as he steered the idling craft to the right side of the harbor. "Fordham, you say? A Jesuit school. It's a very respectable institution," he said looking Mark dead in the eye without blinking, then nodding in approval. "I can see you're telling the truth". He paused and then continued. "There's something I can't put my finger on about you, Straight. You're different than anyone else I've ever met. You're a good, sincere man. Nothing phony about the likes of you. But there's something very, very different about you. I also know you know what it is I'm talking about, though I don't know it more than an intuition."

The craft continued idling along, hugging the right side of the harbor.

"Yes Ernest, I know exactly what you're talking about. I'll tell you something, and that is in good time. When the stars align correctly, I'll fill you in," Mark countered.

"Oh, you're a horse's ass!" Hemingway laughed loudly. "You're going to keep me in suspense, or is this to be a sparring match of wits with me?"

"Ernest, trust me please on this. No, I'm not foolish enough to weigh wits with the likes of you. However, this is a very serious and sensitive subject matter. Please trust me and give me time on it," Mark politely requested.

"Almost sounds like espionage. I'm very intrigued. My guess is that only a handful of people know about what you do and who you are," Hemingway surmised.

Laughing, Mark answered Hemingway humorously. "Well, they know me as a bartender at the Victoria. At least I used to be a bartender there. I resigned not all that long ago because of who and what I am. There is one person I have confided in. That was back in Paris a dozen or more years ago."

"Paris? I was there then and that's where we originally met, it turns out. Who was it? Scott?" Hemingway asked, inquiring if it may have been his friend F. Scott Fitzgerald.

"Ha Ha! With a wife like Zelda? I might as well print it on the front page of the New York Times!"

"That's true. Zelda is a real nut. In all seriousness, she may very well belong in a nuthouse. She doesn't drink well either. She's a sloppy drunk."

Hemingway steered the craft along at idle while continuing his conversation. Josie had been tending to the three wahoo and by doing that, removed himself from the conversation a few minutes earlier.

"How about Pasos?"

"No. I didn't really talk to Pasos all that much. Ok, I'll tell you the one person who knows. You can't send them a letter inquiring. Again, this is extremely sensitive. I'll tell you who it is, providing that person is kept between you and me. I will tell you in time what my situation is, however it's highly confidential and even more highly sensitive. I need your word, Ernest."

He knew from history that Hemingway was always good for his word.

"You have it Mr. Straight," offering his hand to shake. They shook, sealing their bond.

"Gertrude Stein."

"That bitch!"

Mark looked a bit amazed. "When I met you all those years ago, you were good friends. She took you under her wing and acted as a sort of mentor."

"Gertrude and I have our ups and downs. At the moment it's down. It will rise again. Let's make a deal, for the moment. You don't ask me about Gerti and I'll stop inquiring about whatever the hell you are. Fair enough?"

"That works for me," Mark answered, realizing shortly after he said it, that it was not a phrase of the era.

"You see Mark? It's like these odd phrases you use. 'That works for me'. That's not any slang I've ever heard before. Ah! We're at Cuban Customs."

Saved by the bells of Cuban Customs and an absent Gertrude Stein, a double ringer at the nick of time. He escaped on a technicality, but he'd take the win any way he could get it. And win he had. The arrival at Customs took the front seat to what Hemingway saw as a curiosity about Mark.

Funny as it seemed, that fact remained that Ernest Hemingway was indeed a very intuitive individual if there ever was one. However, pondering the obvious would get him nowhere. Just something that Mark saw as a red flag in using Twenty-First Century vernacular in 1935.

Ernest eased Pilar slowly to the dock. Josie tossed the stern line to one of the dock hands and Mark sought refuge from the conversation with Hemingway, scampering up to the bowline, tossing it to another dock hand. He knew at one point or another, he would confide with Hemingway. However, the game now was afoot. They had arrived in Havana.

The lines of Pilar secured at the dock, Josie, Ernest and Mark went to clear customs. The people in the customs office on the dock were well acquainted with Hemingway. That was apparent from the moment he finished docking Pilar. Both dock hands waved as he disembarked and hollering out "¡Ola Señior Hemingway! Como estas?"

Hemingway replied in Spanish to each personally "¡Ola Rodrigo! Ola Jose! ¿Cómo están ambos? ¿Ha estado cuidando de La Habana para mí? " Everybody laughed.

Josie laughed "They love him here! He just asked them if they had taken good care of Havana while he was gone. Ha Ha!"

Hemingway saw Mark starting to dig into his bag. Steve Craig had set him up in his own time with all legal documents before they jumped to 1934.

"Don't worry about a passport, all you need is a U.S. driver license."

The three headed into the Customs Office. Hemingway took the lead. "Gustavo! It's been too long! How are you?" The man came out from behind the counter and embraced Hemingway like an old friend. He was overweight, around sixty and smoking a cigar. His English was quite impressive actually. He had a slight accent, more of a tone actually, and he spoke in a high voice.

"Ah! Señior Hemingway! Welcome back to Cuba! No doubt you are here to enjoy a few bars, nightlife, and some good living again for a few days? By the way, I'm enjoying your collection of short stories

'Winner Take Nothing.' I know it's a couple of years old, but getting literature from outside of Cuba isn't always quick, especially if it's in English. If it were Jorge Guillén from Spain, it would be much more readily available!"

After the quick embrace, he kept a hand on Hemingway's shoulder. It was obvious that they also knew each other outside of the Customs Office.

Taking his hand off of Hemingway's shoulder he addressed Josie. "Mr. Joseph Russell, how have you been?" He said laughing. They shook hands warmly.

Then the customs officer leaned sideways towards Hemingway, speaking out of the side of his mouth in a hush-hush jokingly sort of way, continued, "You have a new arrival with you?" The way he did it reminded Mark of Schultz, on the TV series *Hogan's Heroes,* which wouldn't air for another thirty years. He also reminded him of Lou Costello, in both his appearance and voice. From his mannerisms alone, Mark liked this man.

Hemingway burst out, "Of course Gus, meet our new friend Mark Straight. This man gaffed and hurled those three one-hundred pound wahoo onto the deck, each on a single bound! He's a good man, Gustavo. He even has a degree in English literature and prose from Fordham University. Gustavo Abreu, meet Mark Straight."

They shook hands and Gustavo Abreu continued in his high-pitched voice, "First of all, feel free to call me Gus. Fordham is a highly respected institution. That speaks volumes." He was somehow knowledgeable on American Universities.

At this point, Hemingway interjected. "Careful with him Mark! His English is almost perfect. His parents sent him to a military high school in Georgia. I say almost. Gus doesn't get contractions, but who could find fault in that?"

"Oh, he is right! I cannot get contractions in English. We do not have them in Spanish. My brain does not process them!" Gus replied. Then turning back to Hemingway, he continued "So Ernest, how long will you stay with us and what is your business here in Cuba?" He asked with a sarcastic grin, as though it was a required question to ask, that he very well knew the answer to already.

"Put us in for a week Gus. It will most likely be less. The first order of business is getting these three wahoo on ice over at Marina Pepe's."

"Well then, let's get all of you to sign these documents and be on your way! Perhaps I'll see you tonight at the Floridita?" Gus replied as he returned to the counter and laid out the paperwork to be signed and filled out. "Just put your name and address there, plus your driver license number. Tell us where you'll be staying. Oh, Mr. Hemingway, did you by chance remember to bring me a care package?"

"You know I'd turn around in the middle of the Straits of Florida if I forgot that Gus! Josie grabbed it getting off the boat here. Josie?"

Josie stepped forward with a brown satchel and handed it to Gus. It was clearly heavy. "Three are in there, plus, another bonus from Virginia," Hemingway replied.

"Three! Gracias Sr. Hemingway! You are so kind to a meager government employee on a low income" replied Gus, in a wimpish tone.

Hemingway roared in laughter "Gus! You make more on shall we call 'incentives' at this crazy port than I make monthly writing for Esquire!"

Everyone laughed. It was a most friendly customs house, Mark was thinking, albeit with a few underhanded dealings.

Everyone shook hands and the three left, getting on their boat and heading on to Marina Pepe's Bodega, a little ways down the harbor.

A fifteen-minute idle down the harbor brought them to Marina Pepe's Bodega. The restaurant and harbor were ramshackle at best. Had it been in the U.S. in the twenty-first century, the board of health would have closed it before even entering the driveway.

However, this was Havana, Cuba, and it was 1935. Mark thought, "When in Rome…"

The restaurant/bar/dockmaster's office was a corrugated roof affair. The dockmaster's office was up front, overlooking the marina itself. It was an eight by ten room with upper-mounted storm shutters, which were open by day. The restaurant and bar had no windows or walls for that matter. Wooden tables, secured at the base, all offered a good view of the harbor.

Ernest hopped off the boat and as he passed the dockmaster's office, waved and said hello as he quickly walked past, raising his index finger as to say, "One second please." Again, like the customs house, the dockmaster obviously knew him, nodding and waving back with a big smile and a local greeting. "¡Hola, Señor Hemingway!"

Hemingway headed to the back of the restaurant toward the kitchen. The kitchen was manned by a cheerful black man named Manny who nodded and smiled. While Mark and Josie waited on the dock, they watched them exchange pleasantries, after which it was clear they were discussing the three wahoo. It didn't take long. Together they walked back to Pilar. Hemingway quickly pointed to Mark and only said, "Mark," then he pointed at Manny and said "Manny." Manny smiled and nodded saying, "Mucho gusto," the Spanish cordial when meeting someone for the first time. Then, looking at Josie, said with a thick Cuban accent while waving and nodding "Josie!" pronouncing the J in his name as it is in Spanish. Then he asked to see the fish.

"¿Por favor, muéstrame el pescado?"

Josie opened the well with the three fish in it.

"¡Coño!!! ¡Te doy cuatro centavos la libra!" Many said excitedly.

"Cinco centavos y tenemos un trato," Hemingway countered.

Josie leaned over to Mark and said in his ear, "Manny wants four cents a pound. Ernest just countered with five cents."

"Señor, sólo puedo vender esto a los pescadores locales ya los trabajadores portuarios. No pueden pagarlo si pago cinco centavos. Los hoteles le darán tal vez siete o incluso ocho centavos. ¿Puedo venderles?"

Josie again leaned to Mark with a translation "He says the fishermen and workers here can't afford it at five cents. He says the hotels can offer a lot more and he could try to broker it for him."

Then Hemingway spoke again. "No, muchos, deje el pescado aquí para los trabajadores. Cuatro centavos es." Then he paused and said, "Sin embargo, usted me promete que el pescado a cuatro centavos se queda aquí para los trabajadores. Si usted vende cualquiera a los hoteles, lo vende en ocho centavos, conserve dos centavos para se y déme dos. ¿Justa?"

Josie continued translating to Mark. "He said to keep the fish at four cents so the workers can have it, but if he sells any to the hotels, sell it at eight cents and they'll split the difference."

There was well over three hundred pounds of fish. Chances were that at least one fish would go to the hotels, maybe two. Mark nonetheless, was impressed with Hemingway's generosity and compassion for the workers.

Manny let out a whistle that was nothing short of a shriek and a couple of kitchen hands came running out to assist hauling the big fish back to the kitchen.

Hemingway started to the dockmaster's office, then stopped in his tracks and turned around calling back to Manny, "Una cosa más. ¿Nos puede hacer una cena gratis con los peces por favor?"

"¡Absolutamente!" Manny answered, waving his right arm to Hemingway.

Hemingway pondered for a moment, then called out, "Y tres cervezas cada uno".

"¡Coño¡ ¡Me estás matando! Ok, tres cervezas."

Josie laughed and turned to Mark saying, "We're getting free dinner and three beers each!"

Hemingway then called to Mark, "Come on! You need to meet the dockmaster. If you come here without Josie or me, they'll beat you senseless and throw you in the drink!"

They went up to the Dockmaster's office. The windows took up ninety percent of the walls and each was wide open. The man inside had a dark olive complexion and his skin had the texture of old, worn leather.

Hemingway again took the lead, just as he had done in the customs house.

"Jose! How are you?"

"Ernest, welcome back. I might be able to make room for you, I'm hoping?" Jose answered.

"Well, just like Gus in customs, I have three bottles of one-hundred proof Old Grand Dad, plus a Virginia ham. Now, what are the chances that I can get a slip in this rats nest of yours, or do I have to go visit Jorge at Marino Pelícano?" Hemingway fired back with a smile on his face, though his voice was sincere.

"No problem, no problem!" the dock master getting fidgety, knowing that Hemingway might very well head to the other marina, three one-hundred proof Old Grand Dads and a Virginia ham in tow if pressed anymore.

"That's better. And I don't want a slip out in bum fuck Egypt either. Maybe five to eight slips out." Hemingway was clearly enjoying his victory.

It was a good dock, too. Very quick access to the restaurant and bar, and more importantly, the road out of here to town.

"Jose, I want you to meet Mark Straight. He's with us. Mark, this is the dockmaster, Jose Cifrian."

"¡Mucho gusto y Bienvenidos de Cuba Mark! I hope you'll enjoy your stay here!"

"Thank you. My pleasure." They shook hands and then Josie piped in, "Let's grab those beers and some wahoo! I'm starving!"

Mark turned to Josie and enquired, "Where did you learn Spanish, Key West?"

"I did learn a lot in Key West, no doubt about that. Naturally, I have all sorts of Cuban friends. I perfected it running rum, however. I was the focus of that folklore, believe it or not. I was, in fact, a rum runner. You'd be amazed how fast you can knuckle down on a language when money is involved!" Josie laughed

They all headed to Pilar and moved her to the assigned slip. Once secured, they headed to the restaurant and had an ice cold Cuban lager beer, Hatuey, while they waited for their wahoo dinner. After two Hatueys each, the wahoo was brought out. Manny had marinated it in mojo for 20 minutes then grilled it, having seasoned it with Cuban spices. It came with the standard black beans and rice, as well as yuca. On the side was a Cuban avocado salad. All three agreed that this was a meal to remember for a long, long time. Totally magnificent would be an accurate description.

When the meal was over, they each had a cafecito.

"The dockmaster, Jose, offered to drive us to Hotel Ambos Mundos when we were done." Hemingway offered.

"Hotel Ambos Mundos?" Mark questioned. He had never heard of the hotel, not that he was all that worldly on hotels to begin with. "You know, I found that I was coming here so often, I just said the hell with it. I just keep a room here at the hotel for when I come down. It's number 511. It's set up for my writing as well, so I'm not divorced from my work while I'm here. Josie will pick up what is available there as we visit, as my room will accommodate only one. The rates are reasonable. On the other hand, feel free to stay on Pilar if you're on a budget," Ernest explained.

"I'm very fortunate in that I have the luxury to afford a hotel. If you two are staying at this Hotel Ambos Mundos, I'll do the same."

They went back to Pilar and grabbed their belongings. Jose Cifrian was locking the dockmaster's booth when they returned. They piled into his nineteen-twenty something Model T and headed to the hotel.

Getting out of the old car, Hemingway turned to Jose, shaking his hand. "Thanks for the ride Jose! Be careful with that Ol' Grand Dad, it's one-hundred proof."

They entered the hotel and Mark was indeed impressed. The ceiling in the lobby had to be close to twenty feet tall. The words "stately and airy" came to mind when Mark first walked in. They all checked in. Mark was in room 309 while Josie was in room 212. The concierge knew them both and greeted them warmly, while cordially introducing himself to Mark in English as Nestor Triana de Rodriguez, following that with, "I trust this will be the first of many visits. A friend of Señor Hemingway and Señor Russell is indeed a friend of Hotel Ambos Mundos!" Mark felt as though he'd been here before and felt very good about it.

The three men all went to their respective rooms to shower and rest up for a couple of hours. Hemingway stated that he wanted to go to the bar to see a particular singer that evening, so they all agreed to meet in the lobby at 10 pm.

The hotel had a courtyard, encased with a glass A-frame roof, while below there were all sorts of tropical plants. Mark found his room and went in. He found it was quite comfortable. All day on the Straits of Florida and catching three wahoo had taken its toll. A warm bath would be in order.

He actually fell asleep in the tub and woke up startled. Quickly running out of the bathroom with a quick toweling off, he was relieved to see he still had twenty minutes before meeting Ernest and Josie in the lobby. He dressed quickly and was in the lobby five minutes early. Josie and Ernest were already there.

"You're early! A good attribute of a man with conviction," Hemingway stated almost in a military tone. Of course, he was unaware that Mark was sound asleep in the tub twenty minutes ago. Let sleeping dogs lie, Mark thought.

Hemingway motioned to the door and as the three casually walked to the door, Hemingway continued, "We're heading to one of my favorite bars. It's only four blocks down the street so it's convenient and within walking distance. It's the Floridita Bar. A Spaniard named Constante owns it. He himself invented the Daiquiri there. As a mixologist, you might find him an interesting individual."

"He invented the Daiquiri? Really?"

"Yes, this is a frozen one. There is another from the province of Oriente that has ice cubes. I much prefer Constante's. As for myself, I'm looking forward to hearing the woman who sings in the bar. It's the perfect combination of a good drink and a woman singing. They have a guitar, a bass, and percussion, and the vocalist who accompanies them singing is a woman whom I find quite enchanting," Ernest replied.

"Oh?" Mark replied. Josie laughed.

"Not in a romantic way. No. Her voice, however, paints the pictures of the stories of the songs she is singing in the most descriptive way with elegant style and grace. What she sings is the essence of Cuba itself."

"That's impressive, especially coming from you. What is her name?" Mark inquired as they walked down the street.

"Mercedes Eguizabal. She's of Basque stock. I know her well and have spoken with her many times. Her grandparents came from the Pyrenees in Spain. A curious people indeed. The Basque language is not related to Spain or France, the countries in which they live. Some say they are the survivors of Atlantis. They are a feisty people, so I wouldn't doubt that at all."

There's nothing on the planet that beats folklore, Mark was thinking.

There was a blue sign ahead at the end of the street which read, "Restaurante Bar Floridita."

They entered the bar off Calle Obispo. There was a moderate crowd.

"Let's find a table," Hemingway said as they entered and made their way through the bar. The band was playing a slow, Cuban lament. Mark could make out that is was that of a lover who had left the country for the city and now the woman was alone. The Spanish word "triste", which meant "sad," returned in the chorus of the song. As they moved through the bar four men got up from the bar itself. Timing was perfect and Hemingway took a middle seat while Josie and Mark sat on either side of him. An empty seat waited for another patron. La Floradita was an old bar. It was a small, classic, and elegant bar. Like the Hotel Ambos Mundos, the ceilings were quite high. Not as high as the hotel, but easily around fourteen feet high.

Hemingway greeted the bartender and they shook hands like old friends, most likely because they were. After pleasantries, Hemingway ordered three daiquiris. He turned to Mark and motioned to the bartender. "This is my friend Mark. Mark, this is Martin Eloriaga, one of the finest bartenders in all of Cuba. He was tutored by the owner, Constante, the patron himself of the Daiquiri. If Constante trusts him, he's good in our book. No one is better than Constante himself."

Martin Eloriaga greeted Mark formally and cordially, with a proper handshake and a nod. "Mucho Gusto, Señor." He was an elegant man dressed in a tuxedo and a bow tie. After greeting Mark he swiftly went about his business of making the mixed drinks. He may have been the best, however, he was also quite busy.

Mark and Hemingway turned on their stools at the bar, joining Josie in watching the crowd and the music. The band was playing by the front door, which was a smart way to lure passers by into the establishment.

Something funny caught Mark's attention in a very odd sort of way. Getting his perch at the bar squared away, he then looked at the singer of the Cuban quartette, Mercedes Eguizabal. "Holy Shit!" he thought without hesitation. She was in the middle of a song when she saw him, and though she never lost a beat, her eyes opened wide. Very wide.

"You say you know this singer Ernest?"

"Very well actually." The daiquiris were delivered and the three toasted.

"Salud!" they all said, toasting their glasses.

Hemingway took a hard drink of the frozen daiquiri, then turned to Mark saying, "Yes. Señora Mercedes Eguizabal and I are close confidants. There are things she knows of me that never will be repeated and one very unusual and oddly interesting thing about her that I am sworn to never divulge."

Mark looked at the singer once again and she looked at him, this time in a knowingly, cautious, and curious way. At the end of the song, Mark now nodded to her. She paused, never losing eye contact with him, then slowly, nodded back. The guitar player started a new song after quiet applause of the audience and she started a bolero.

Mark turned to Ernest. "You said you and she share confidences?"

"We do."

"Ernest, she's a time traveler."

Hemingway said nothing, but he looked at Mark dead in the eye, with absolutely no expression on his face. Several seconds went by and Ernest continued looking at Mark, saying nothing.

"Yes, Ernest, she's a time traveler." He paused, then continued as the band was in an upbeat number.

"I'm a time traveler as well."

Ernest just looked at him with no expression whatsoever. However, through the quick bustle at the bar and Mercedes and the band playing, Ernest just stared at Mark. Josie, flanking Ernest on his other side, never caught any of the conversation. Far too much chattering, laughing, music, and blenders making daiquiris, for anything to be heard in a conversation taking place two bar stools away.

After around twenty seconds of expressionless, self-imposed mute conversation, Ernest contributed to the cacophony of sound with an observational statement of his own, at a volume that cut through the joyous jubilee, though not. "I told you they were a good band."

It was a telltale move. In changing the subject, Ernest was virtually admitting that he knew Mercedes Eguizabal was a time traveler himself. The subject of being a time traveler was just far too extraordinary to just brush off. He might have just as well asked Mark for the time on his Roskopf.

Mark raised his glass to Ernest and cheered, then leaned over and toasted Josie as well. Ernest, by his own statement, had given his word to Mercedes Eguizabal and that word was good. Mark knew that the subject of himself being a time traveler would rise again, albeit in a private conversation with Ernest, some time subsequently. When that would be, who knows? However, his bonded word would be respected. Mark would not encroach on the subject of Mercedes Eguizabal being a time traveler.

The daiquiris continued to flow and the band played on, while the crowd was joyous and laughing throughout. La Floridita, circa 1935 was a fun night spot indeed!

After forty-five minutes of their arrival, the three caballeros downed four daiquiris each, at which point the band took a break. Mercedes Eguizabal came over and warmly greeted Ernest and Josie in Spanish.

Ernest then introduced her to Mark in Spanish. Mark's Spanish was enough to get them through the cordials of introduction, however, if they were to broach the subject of something like how a tobacco plantation is run, he'd be entirely lost. He tried to keep it simple.

"¡Tienes una gran voz! ¡Me encantó! ¿Es usted de La Habana?" He asked.

"Thank you! No, I'm from the city of Cienfuegos, on the south side of the island," Mercedes answered in perfect English, with a distinctly American accent.

Ernest then burst in laughing. "Wait a minute! You speak English! All this time I've been speaking to you in Spanish. It's at least a couple of years. I had no clue that you spoke English!"

"Well, surprise!" Then motioning to Mark, "Also, between the three of us, Ernest, he knows. You're off the hook and have the liberty to talk about what we are, so long as it's between the three of us. Time travelers can tell each other in an instant, by the way. When our eyes met we instantly knew we were both travelers. Regarding my English, I've spent many, many years in the U.S. In future times, mind you. So, of course, I speak English. By the way, I also speak Italian, German, and can get by okay in French."

"Well, I'll be a horse's ass!" Hemingway laughed.

Turning to Mercedes, Mark said, "I've never met a woman time traveler before. I'd love to talk more about it, but this isn't the time or place."

"You're right about this not being the right time or place. Perhaps we could meet for coffee in the morning?"

That sounds good. How's the lobby of my hotel? I'm at Hotel Ambos Mundos. Say, 10 am?"

"That's good, or if you like we could have breakfast and coffee here at the Floridita?"

"That's even better!"

The band break was over and Mercedes went back on stage. Mark found something new this evening at La Floridita bar in Havana. The fact that he met his first woman time traveler, was the icing on the cake. The real revelation, however, was that he knew immediately that she was a time traveler.

It had been a very long and exciting day. They left Key West early in the morning, trawled the Florida Straits catching three wahoo, arrived in Havana Harbor, docked, ate a fabulous dinner dockside, booked into the Hotel Ambos Mundos, took a good long bath, headed out to La Floridita Bar, had a few daiquiris, listened to some great music, and met a fellow time traveler. Throughout the day he had discretely taken pictures of all of it with his iPhone as well. On top of everything else, here he was living life with Ernest Hemingway and Josie Russell.

Both Ernest and Josie looked as tired as Mark felt. All agreed it was time to call it a night and headed back to the hotel to turn in.

Mark's alarm on his iPhone went off at 8:50. His body ached a bit from the previous day's activity on the boat. He hadn't gaffed a fish in years, and here he'd been gaffing three one-hundred plus pound wahoo and hurling them onto the boat. He likened it to riding a bicycle, although, after around twenty years, the unused muscles felt the burden on this morning after.

He opened the curtains to find a beautiful morning in Havana. The sun was shining and Calle Obispo was active with people walking, vendors selling fruits and vegetables. He opened the window and took in the air of the Havana morning. There was salt in the air from the sea and it was good. He went back in after a few minutes and drew a hot bath.

Laying in the hot water eased the muscle pain considerably. Mark felt fully refreshed after a half hour. He got dressed and headed down the street to La Floridita to meet this new time traveler whom he had met. He snapped some pictures discreetly with his iPhone, making sure no one was looking at him.

He arrived at 9:55 and found Mercedes already waiting at a table for him. Mercedes rose and they exchanged greetings in both Spanish and English. As soon as they sat back down the waiter came and they ordered coffees to start. "Un con leche por favor," Mark requested after Mercedes ordered a cortadito for herself. The waiter looked at him with a funny look and a smile saying "¡Eres de Cayo Hueso! Sólo la gente de Cayo Hueso dice 'con leche.'" (You're from Key West! Only people from Key West say con leche.)

Mercedes laughed and said, "Here in Havana it's always café con leche."

The waiter then replied, "Nuestro nombre local para su ciudad es La Habana Norte," and laughed, then in fun, saluted, as he went to put the order in. Mark didn't understand him but smiled nonethcless.

Mercedes realized this and said to him "What he's saying is that the local name for Key West in Havana is Havana North!"

Key West, or in its Spanish name, Cayo Hueso, in earlier years had been an island where Cuban fishermen would process their fish. They nicknamed it Havana North.

Mark then turned to Mercedes and broke the ice quickly. It was just that first glance encounter where he had that unmistakable knowledge that she was another time traveler. Today, she came across as anyone else would. The revelation was complete and the air let out of the balloon, so to speak. She was around his age, black wavy hair, very dark brown eyes, possibly even black, she stood about 5'3" and weighed around 110. She had a warm smile.

"So, how long have you been a time traveler?" Mark inquired.

"About five years. We have a good, very supportive branch of the organization here in Havana. I was very fortunate to have them here to guide me into the lifestyle," she answered.

"Are you in your own time now, or are you traveling?"

"I'm traveling. I was born in 1975 in Cienfuegos, Cuba. In my real time, I'm living in Miami."

"I must admit, you're the first time traveler I met who is a woman." Mark half stated, half questioning.

Mercedes laughed, "How long have you been traveling?"

"Not very long, actually," Mark replied.

"You will find, in time, that there are as many women time traveling, as there are men. It's kind of like conception. One male, one female. There may be slightly more men, but it's a trivial amount. You will meet more, in time!" she laughed, adding, "Pun intended!"

Mark very much enjoyed Mercedes' disposition. She was smart, the requiem for time travelers, yet jovial at the same time.

The waiter returned with the two café orders and as they consumed their coffees, they touched on each other's backgrounds. Mercedes had always been an art student, then professor, having studied and taught in Italy, Spain, and Germany over the years. She got into music quite by chance.

"I was at a jazz club in Paris and the singer became ill. They had a few more numbers to go and asked if anyone in the audience knew 'Girl From Ipanema.' I'm a big Jobim fan and can pretty much get by in Portuguese. I knew the song and the rest is history. These days I travel to Paris to sing, as well as here. I don't sing at all in my own time, funny enough."

"Where and when in Paris?" There was excitement in Mark's voice when he enquired.

"Early 1920's" She replied. Then added "That's how I know Ernest. We've met there and here before."

"Holy crap! I've been there in that same time period, but only met Ernest in a passing-by situation back then. We've become friends in this time period however," Mark explained.

"Would you like a word of advice, if I may offer one?" Mercedes asked.

"By all means! Pray tell. Continue."

"If you should go back to the early 1920's, use caution with Ernest. You've established your bond and friendship with him here twelve or fifteen years later. If you do anything with him in that time period again, be advised that you will be changing history with your friendship. These things can very easily backfire in a very bad way. If Ernest took you on this trip, he likes, trusts, and respects you, correct?"

"Yes, it's mutual, as you might imagine."

"Good! Keep it that way. If Ernest gets to know you at this stage in the 1920's, that changes the history of what happens when he meets you again in 1935. Ernest can be volatile, as you know. If things go bad between you in the 1920's, you and I will never have had this conversation this morning, because he may have never taken you on this trip to Havana."

"Holy crap! I never thought of it that way."

What a revelation! Sure, if he had an altercation with a drunk, volatile Hemingway in the 1920's, when he saw Mark in Sloppy Joe's the first time, he might have just spat on the floor and walked away when he saw him. Mark thought "When I go back to Paris, I'll avoid contact with Ernest."

It wasn't a matter of if, but when. He loved Paris, had a room there, as well as a friend whom he entrusted his secret with, Gertrude Stein. Plus, now he had an interest in seeing Mercedes, a fellow time traveler, sing in Paris.

"I definitely want to see you sing in Paris, Let's set up a date and time!"

"Oh, well, just to set the stage, I'm married."

"I knew right away from your ring. I have only artistic intentions. As a matter of fact, I have a girlfriend in 1935 Key West right now."

"Really? Does she know you are a time traveler?"

"No. It gets weirder than that though. My mentor is also from our time and has a family in 1935. I was meaning to look further into that when Ernest invited me on this trip. So, I have an agenda when we get back."

"What? His normal time is the same as ours and he has a family in 1935? You're kidding, right?" Mercedes said, wide eyed and horrified.

"That's the way I understand it. I didn't hear about this until a few days ago. I haven't had time to inquire with him about it yet," Mark explained.

"I've never heard of such a thing, other than someone choosing to live in another time, in which case they are in a loop. You've perhaps heard of Brian Fields?"

"Indeed I have. As a matter of fact, Brian Fields was explained and shown to me by the very same mentor we're talking about. Like I say, I'm very curious to talk with him now. I will after we get back to Key West, be it now in 1935, or in our own time."

"I'm very curious about this. Please keep me posted!" Mercedes replied, still in a state of amazement.
"Agreed. I'd like to catch your show in Paris, perhaps we could hook up there and I could update you?"

"That's a plan!" Mercedes burst out. Then, laughing she asked, "Are you interested in my 21st Century show, or my 1935 show?"

They made arrangements for their natural time, then finished their coffee and conversation. As they departed La Floridita, Mercedes said with a friendly smile "My Friends call me Mercy, by the way. Hasta luego," using the common Cuban salutation for saying goodbye. Translated it literally means "until then."

Mark was deep in thought as he headed back to Hotel Ambos Mundos. He pulled out and looked at his Roskopf watch. It read 11:54 and he wondered, heading to rendezvous with Ernest and

Josie, "Ironic, isn't it? When is ' until then', after all? Is it in the future, or has it already happened?"

When Mark walked into the lobby of Hotel Ambos Mundos, he found Ernest sitting in one of the luxurious chair and table sets adorning the room almost randomly, in the large open area in front of the concierge desk. They were in sets of three and were made from a very light colored thick bamboo. The cushions were a bright tropical floral pattern in green, blue, yellow, and red. In front of them were round wooden coffee tables.

At first, Ernest didn't notice as Mark approached. He was absorbed in a book titled "The Open Boat" by Stephen Crane. Mark sat in one of the chairs at the table and Ernest suddenly looked up. "Oh! Straight! Sorry, I was lost in this book. I should know better than to read in a hotel lobby. However, we also have the arrangement to meet here. Josie's here as well. He just went up the street to the newsstand to pick up the New York Times. It's flown in every day. Great paper. Myself, while I'm here I read Dario de la Marina. It's a paper with fortitude. They go after the government."

Ernest laughed. Mark noted that for the first time, Ernest had called him by his last name. In most cases, it worked the other way around. One might refer to someone by their last name until a degree of familiarity set in. With his case, Ernest worked the opposite. Mark felt good that he had called him by his last name.

Ernest continued. "You met with Mercedes this morning?"

"Indeed I did. We had a nice time and got to know each other a bit more. I'm looking forward to seeing her again, as a matter of fact," Mark replied.

"Let's get to the meat of the matter here, as it's just you and me. You're both time travelers. She told me under oath and that naturally extends to you, Mark Straight," Ernest stated, offering his handshake as his bond while looking him dead in the eye. Here was the essence of the word earnest, coming directly from none other than Ernest Hemingway himself.

"Thank you, Ernest. Discretion is paramount. You already know that from Mercedes. I'm actually new to all of this. For me, it all started not very long ago, so I'm still feeling my way around it. There's a shipload of things that I still have to learn. She advised me that should I go back to 1920's Paris to avoid you. If our relationship grew any more than it did back then, at this stage, it could potentially change everything. Think about it Ernest, if we had more interactions back then, there's a possibility that you and I would not be seated in the lobby of the Hotel Ambos Mundos talking right now."

Ernest lowered his eyebrows in very serious thought for several seconds. "Interesting point there, Straight. You're right on all counts. I agree fully. If you go back there, ignore me. Like yourself, I like things as they are."

"Agreed," Mark replied, this time offering his hand to seal the bond.

At this point, a bellhop wearing a fez approached them saying in perfect English, "Gentlemen, I apologize for the interruption. I see you shaking hands a lot, so I know you're in a business meeting, but can I get you some refreshment?"

Mark and Ernest both laughed. "I guess it is a business matter of sorts. I think we're okay, however, Manuel. We have plans. Oh, here's Josie now," Hemingway said, addressing the hotel employee. As he kept a room there year 'round, naturally he knew the entire staff. Mark admired how Hemingway addressed people. It never mattered if it was the head of a firm, or, in this case, a bellhop wearing a fez. Ernest always treated everyone with the same respect.

Josie approached with the paper in his hands. "Ready for lunch, gentlemen?" he asked, walking at a fast clip across the lobby towards the two seated gentlemen.

"Well, I am! How about you Mark?" Ernest inquired.

"I'm in! Where are we off to? You two know the lay of the land here. I'm an outsider," Mark replied.

"We're off to Sloppy Joe's!" Josie exclaimed with the excitement of a man twenty years younger.

"Sloppy Joe's? But that's your bar in Key West," Mark stated, a bit puzzled.

Ernest and Josie laughed together, while Mark remained confused, but managed a smile, knowing there was a story here.

"The Sloppy Joe's here was the first Sloppy Joe's. A Spaniard named Jose Qabael Otero opened it. Way back, there was always ice melting from the fish storage and the floors were wet. Hence, the Sloppy Joe's name. We started coming here during prohibition. Josie was a rum runner from way back! They have a good Ropa Vieja there, plus they distill their own rum. I suggested to Josie that he name his bar Sloppy Joe's. As his name is Joseph, it fit."

"Let's go! I'm ready for a damned mojito!" Josie proclaimed laughing.

"The game's afoot! It's time to roll!" Mark proclaimed and the three hustled out the front door.

"Conan-Doyle! I'm glad you're not an author Straight. I'd hate your ass!" Hemingway blurted out, half in jest, half serious.

Everyone laughed and headed down the street.

It wasn't too long a walk, only several blocks, but less than fifteen minutes. When they arrived, Ernest and Josie were in their element. It seemed they knew everyone in the bar and everyone in the bar knew them. There was a lot of back-slapping, and roars of laughter, enhanced by the atmosphere and the loud cacophony of sound that permeated within the bar.

Mark was actually surprised with the bar. It could have easily been on Park Avenue, in New York City rather than Havana, Cuba. Posh was a good way to describe it. It seemed the patrons were all drinking mojitos, daiquiris, or beer. No wine glasses were seen anywhere, while perhaps a half dozen martinis were to be counted in a crowd of perhaps one hundred.

On the whole, Hemingway was not a table man. For him, it was always the bar. At least this was the case when he was out with his male friends. When he was out with Pauline, it was a different story.

Mark was noting that when Hemingway entered a bar, the crowd at the bar would part, as the Red Sea did for Moses. It happened at La Floridita Bar and it did likewise in Key West, at Sloppy Joe's. The seas just parted and Ernest made his way to the bar. It was uncanny, actually.

Mark's memory went back to Paris on the evening that he met F. Scott Fitzgerald and his wife Zelda. He was comparing authors in bars suddenly. What a contrast! The Fitzgeralds were table people. Perhaps that had something to do with why Hemingway thought Zelda was nuts. That was months ago, or was it years? His reasoning was both.

Of course, like the night before at La Floridita, the bar cleared for Hemingway. Mark couldn't help but chuckle to himself.

"I'm going to call you Moses from now on, I think," Mark stated frankly.

"Moses?" Hemingway asked.

Josie caught the analogy immediately and roared with laughter. He then burst out "That's perfect! Moses! I love it!" he announced as he made a motion with his two arms of the parting of the Red Sea. "Moses! Yes!"

Ernest laughed and sounded off. "If you guys start calling me Moses, we'll take it outside and I'll not only beat you both to a pulp, but I'll leave you sorry butts here in Cuba to fend for yourselves!"

Everyone laughed and Ernest turned to the bartender, holding three fingers up and said, "Nestor, tres mojitos por favor!"

Nestor Triana was a man in his early thirties, impeccably dressed in a black jacket and matching pants, with a white shirt and a black bow tie. Nestor was the head bartender that day. Ernest knew him well, apparently. His reply was in English. "Immediately Ernest!" The fact that he used his first name was a giveaway of their familiar nature.

Suddenly Gus Abreu, the head customs officer they met the previously the day before on their entrance to Havana, flew into the bar with an enormous grin on his face.

"Hemingway, Russell, and Straight! Funny meeting you here!"

Ernest gave a slight wave as Gus Abreu walked rapidly to them at the bar, then turned to the bartender saying "Make that four mojitos Nestor!" Then turned back to the approaching customs director.

Out of the side of his mouth, Hemingway said to Mark, " 'Funny meeting us here? What a load of crap!"

Mark intermediately thought there might some sort of customs issue. "Oh shit, is there a problem with customs?" he replied to Hemingway, as Gus shook hands with Josie Russell.

"Problem? Hell no! Gus is a very jovial guy who knows when the cash cow comes to town. He always takes the following day off and we meet here. I buy him lunch and drinks... Hello, Gus! Funny meeting us here? That's a good one!"

In his alto voice, minus contractions, Gus replied "It is funny indeed. The following day you always seem to arrive is my day off, and this is my watering hole, as you Yankees call it! You seem to always be here!" he said winking. "I always see you here as well!" He said with a curious look, and taking his index finger and middle finger,

262

touching just below his eyes, then spinning them around and with the two fingers pointing them at Hemingway and Russell, his head lowered and his eyes looking up with a very inquisitive look. It is a very Cuban gesture. Not something you would see an American do, but quite self-explanatory. The gesture was one you would expect an inspector to use and Gustavo Abreu was indeed an inspector.

Hemingway turned to Mark, laughing under his breath. "This is all a just a show. We do it every time we come here. Did you see the forward berth of Pilar? When we left Key West?"

"Forward berth? Not really. I noticed you had what I'm guessing was boxes under a tarp. Why?" Mark replied.

"You did notice no one in Customs really inspected the boat?" Hemingway asked.

"I saw some of their guys on it when we were in the Customs dock masters office."

"It's all a show. They act like they're checking the boat, but they're really not. We had twenty-five cases of Old Grand Dad, 100 proof in the bow berth. Gus has buyers for it. We docked the boat at Pepe's Marina and Gus's people unloaded it at night. Josie actually buys it through his bar in Key West. He sells it to Gus at a small profit, and I imagine Gus sells it to high end restaurants. It's funny. Josie used to buy rum from the Cubans during prohibition. He made his money as a rum runner. Today he sells them whiskey! It pretty much pays for the gas, lodgings, food, and drink to and fro while we're here. Hell, it pays for both of our apartments here!"

Gus then pulled out a check, handing it to Josie stating "Mr. Russell, you may as well consider this coin of the realm. Banco Nacional will convert it directly to cash on your demand. It's always a pleasure doing business with you."

Smuggling partners with the Customs House. Does it get any crazier than that?

"Josie's virtually in the clear with this. While we don't declare it, they inspect the boat, so the burden is on them, from a legal standpoint.They even stamp each bottle as tax paid," Hemingway declared.

Mark was amazed. They wave the loaded boat through customs, then have a crew empty the cargo at a different marina at night and even give each bottle a tax stamp.

At this point Gus leaned toward Nestor, then in English for emphasis, obviously making a point, asked, "Nestor, could I have an Old Grand Dad one hundred on the rocks, please?"

Everyone laughed loudly at the inside joke. Gus was smiling ear to ear. He was clearly someone who loved life. At this moment, what could be better? He just bought twenty-five cases of Tennessee whisky, sold it at a substantial profit, and now was laughing and drinking it for free in one of Havana's most prestigious bars. Not only that, but Ernest was paying for it. Yes, for Gus Abreu, life right now couldn't be better. This was Gus Abreu's Dolce Vida indeed.

Ernest turned to Mark and inquired, "Are you hungry? Their ropa vieja is outstanding, and their picadillo sandwich is famous."

"Picadillo sandwich? That sounds pretty much like a Sloppy Joe!" a startled Mark replied.

"You know the Sloppy Joe sandwich? They do have them at the bar in Key West actually. Joe started making them, then somehow they started making them here in Havana. This is the first Sloppy Joe's, but Josie has the first Sloppy Joe sandwich. The Key West version is the original. Jose, the owner here, will tell you that point blank. However, theirs is excellent!" explained Ernest.

Mark ordered the Sloppy Joe sandwich and it arrived within five minutes. He didn't realize how hungry he had become and had finished the sandwich rapidly. Now, he was stuffed. A good walk was in order. He told everyone that he'd catch up with them a little later.

It was a jovial atmosphere with everyone laughing and telling stories in both English and Spanish as he left. Walking down the various streets, Mark finally found himself at the famous Malecon, the seafront esplanade of Havana. Across to the right, he saw the castle entrance to the harbor that they had entered only the day before. It seemed so much more than just a day. The second view from this angle was equally as impressive.

Mark sat on the wall and pondered his new found life, which somehow been bestowed on him. Here he was in Havana, sitting on the wall of the Malecon, and it was 1935. He had a girlfriend across the Florida Straits in Key West in this time period as well. He had earned the trust, respect, and friendship of none other than Ernest Hemingway, as well as Josie Russell. Curiosity was at hand finding out that his sponsor, Arthur, had a family in 1935. Why wasn't he in a loop like Brian Fields? He could never forget Paris! He now had intentions of heading back to catch Mercedes Eguizabal sing in a club there, this time in the early 1920's. Naturally, he'd have to see Gertrude Stein on the trip. He recalled bringing her to his time at Hemingway's house in Key West. He liked and trusted Gertrude. In his own time, maybe Blackheart would like to go back again. How was Steve Craig's Duesenberg today? On top of everything, finances were not a concern.

There were all sorts of things to do and unanswered questions. The mystery of time traveling persisted but, with no answers at hand, was it really worth investigating? Or, was it better to go with the flow? All the time travelers he met felt the latter. Mark did as well. At this moment, sitting on the wall at the Malecon in 1935 pondering everything he'd experienced as a time traveler, the change in scenery suited him just fine. It was a little vacation he needed to gather his thoughts and let the experiences of these last weeks sink in. There certainly was a lot to ponder. In a day or two Ernest, Josie, and himself would take Pilar back to Key West. Again he would be traversing the Florida Straits aboard Pilar with Ernest Hemingway and Josie Russell, his new friends. When he returned, there would be a lot of unfinished affairs to look into and others to be finalized. New adventures, he was sure, would be on the horizon.

The one thing he had learned, without exception, was that the time to live is now, no matter what time period he was in. He hopped off the wall and headed for Pepé's Marina. He was thinking of getting better acquainted with the dockmaster there, Jose Cifrian. Then he'd check out Pilar and make sure she was ready for the trip, get the rods and reels set and ready to go because, who knows? In all likelihood, there could be another wahoo in the future, and they needed to be prepared.

Preparedness was Mark's way. A lot of that came from being a bartender. Everything had to be in its place and at the ready. One had to be expecting the unexpected at any given moment. At both the bar and aboard Pilar, this was the modus-operandi. Perhaps it was the same in everything in life as well. There was a lot at stake in his future and in his past and Mark, like the Pilar, needed to be ready.

About the Author:

Key West Chris Rehm is a songwriter, musician, entertainer, beer hound, F-1 and Indy race car fan as well as an author. He has lived in Key West, Florida, since 2008 and loves the Florida Keys! This is his second book. Make sure you follow Mark Straight's further time traveling adventures in Key West Chris's upcoming books.

Be sure to check out Key West Chris Rehm's first book Bar Stories! Available on Amazon/Kindle! Click the link below:

http://amzn.to/2xGctC9

68184788R00149

Made in the USA
Lexington, KY
05 October 2017